A Candlelight Ecstasy Romance™

HER LIPS PARTED IN UNCONSCIOUS INVITATION

The storm outside was building in intensity, but she barely heard it, her heart beating out the sounds of the thunder, the wind just a whisper compared to the rapid inhale and exhale of her breath. Inside, a sensual storm was building in them both that blocked out everything else.

They were aware only of each other. Nothing that surrounded them mattered. It had been the same the first time they had seen each other that day at the speedway, when all the people, the noises, had been blotted out.

THE METAL MISTRESS

Barbara Cameron

A CANDLELIGHT ECSTASY ROMANCE™

Published by
Dell Publishing Co., Inc.
1 Dag Hammarskjold Plaza
New York, New York 10017

For Sue Tomlinson, Jacqueline Fout, and with special
thanks to Elaine Raco Chase

Dell ® TM 681510, Dell Publishing Co., Inc.

Candlelight Ecstasy Romance™ is a trademark of
Dell Publishing Co., Inc., New York, New York.

ISBN: 0-440-15636-X

Printed in the United States of America

First printing—June 1982

Dear Reader:

In response to your continued enthusiasm for Candlelight Ecstasy Romances™, we are increasing the number of new titles from four to six per month.

We are delighted to present sensuous novels set in America, depicting modern American men and women as they confront the provocative problems of modern relationships.

Throughout the history of the Candlelight line, Dell has tried to maintain a high standard of excellence, to give you the finest in reading enjoyment. It is now and will remain our most ardent ambition.

Anne Gisonny
Editor
Candlelight Romances

PROLOGUE

AMERICAN RACER
KILLED IN
FIERY CRASH

MILAN, ITALY (AP)—American auto racing driver Richard Lansing died in a flaming crash in Sunday's Grand Prix of Italy—Formula 1 event.

Lansing appeared to lose control as he came out of a turn soon after the start of the Italian Grand Prix at Monza. Track officials said the car was so badly damaged that they were unable to determine the cause of the crash.

A veteran of both American and international racing circuits, Lansing was considered to be one of the world's great drivers.

Born in Lubbock, Texas, Lansing is survived by his wife and daughter.

CHAPTER ONE

The sound began as a drone, became a jetlike whine, then a hoarse scream as the lone race car slammed down the course. Shock waves of sound and vibration reverberated through the metal tunnel beneath the asphalt track, startling the young woman perched nervously on the backseat of the taxi rushing through the dark womblike passage.

For a moment Jaclyn was suspended in the terrifying clamor and darkness. After an interminable time the light at the end of the tunnel became brighter, and she was borne into the sunfilled familiarity of the infield.

The persistent whine of the racer making continuous circuits around the track wound a constricting cord of tension around Jaclyn's nerves as she left the cab and paid the driver. The sound was a disturbingly familiar one, filling her with a sense of hopeful anticipation yet dread, recalling memories she had so desperately tried to lock away in oblivion.

The roaring din of motors revving up and the terse instructions of the men working on them; the pungent odors of burning fuel and rubber searing on the track; the shifting kaleidoscope of color in the crowd moving about; the mounting tension of the qualifying runs that would determine which cars entered the race that weekend—

Jaclyn's senses reeled under the impact of the incredible spectacle before her.

This was the Daytona International Speedway, scene of America's twice-around-the-clock endurance race.

Her heart pounded faster as she approached hesitantly the gates of the pit area, her eyes swiveling to watch the progress of the race car.

Metal clashed on metal as the driver downshifted and missed a gear, a sickening, grinding noise as frightening as the sound of someone's misstep as they descend a flight of stairs. She cringed, watching the car veer too fast, too sharp into the turn and plunge into the curve. The racer skimmed close, too close to the concrete retaining wall, but the driver miraculously regained control and swung it safely out of the turn and on into the straightaway.

"Just kissed the wall, that one," a spectator remarked. "You want in, miss?"

Jaclyn jerked to attention, finally exhaling the breath she'd been holding, realizing that she stood before the guard at the pit gates. "What? Oh, yes," she said, showing her press pass.

The guard took it indifferently, not noticing the white knuckles of her hand. He glanced at the pass quickly, handed it back to her, and held the gate open. She stood for a moment in indecision.

"Well, aren't you coming in?" he asked a trifle impatiently.

Straightening her shoulders, Jaclyn nodded and stepped confidently inside. "Do you know where the Spinnelli team—" she began to ask, but the guard's attention was already on another car making its qualifying run.

Never mind, she thought. It's taken me four years to

9

summon up courage to enter another racetrack. Finding my friends should be easy.

Concrete stalls lined pit road, each cubicle crammed with a race car, enough parts seemingly to make another, and hordes of mechanics and others. Confronted by a bewildering lineup of cars and people, Jaclyn searched in vain for the driver friends she had come to interview for a magazine article.

Finally she stopped beside a burnt-orange racer. While mechanics worked on it, a young man was lovingly wiping all traces of oil and grease from the cars stylish paint, almost caressing it with his polishing cloth.

"Can you help me?" she asked, but he moved away, intent on a speck near the front fender.

Frowning at his lack of attention, she turned as someone moved past her quickly, carrying a tire. "Excuse me, I'm looking for—" she began, but he, too, seemed not to hear.

Next she tried a coveralled mechanic who was walking by: "Can you tell me where I can find—"

Ignored. Totally ignored.

Anywhere else her cool blond beauty, her long-legged grace, would have attracted male notice, offers of help. She smiled, but it wasn't that rare, slow smile that lit her finely boned features, dazzling the lucky onlooker, but the one tinged with bitterness and a trace of sullenness that she had worn years before in a similar scene. Her eyes were emerald-dark with memory as she stood unnoticed among the surrounding hive of activity, her honey-gold hair blowing in the warm breeze of a Florida spring, remembering . . .

This was the place where the metal mistress reigned supreme, where no woman, however beautiful or desirable or in need of aid, could attract the attention lavished upon the painted and polished temptress known as the race car. Here was her boudoir, where she enticed men with her deep-throated purring and chrome curves.

Hers was the sultry voice attracting attention, her bodily ills instantly attended by mechanics with all the dedication and skill of the finest surgeons. Her troubles were the only ones receiving sympathy from these men.

It mattered little to those seduced into worshiping her that their efforts might be in vain; that their long hours of toil might be wasted if a small part in her anatomy failed, or other cars were faster or more admired by the all-important fans.

And for the man who sought eagerly the privilege of driving her, it was unimportant that the apple offered by this Eve was deadly. With it often came the inevitable consequence of a painful death or disfigurement if their bodies were smashed in a jumble of metal and flesh upon the racetrack.

Her seductive promise of speed and adventure lured men, her bait—fame and fortune. With his driver/lover's hands at her controls, the man and his mistress gave their all to reach their mutual passion, seeking the breathless climax of victory.

Jaclyn paused for a moment and struggled to recall when she had first heard a race car being referred to as a metal mistress. It had been many years ago, she remembered, when she was a child, that she had first heard the expression. She'd overheard her mother telling a friend that Jaclyn's father was out of town again, and the woman had asked if he was with his metal mistress.

Jaclyn, about to enter the room to ask a question, saw her mother frown. She listened curiously, hoping to find out what a metal mistress was. But her mother had seen her, and she was promptly sent away before her curiosity could be satisfied.

Metal mistress. What on earth was that? Jaclyn had wondered. And why had her mother been so upset? Wait, she'd thought. It sounded familiar. Hadn't she seen something in her elementary school history book about it? Yes, there it was, on page forty-three.

No, no it wasn't. She looked closer. This was something called an iron maiden, a huge, grotesquely shaped metal object.

> Shaped like a sarcophagus, this grisly torture device was used in medieval times. Opened, it revealed long, deadly spikes. When closed, the iron maiden enveloped a man inside her metal arms and impaled him from within, swiftly, fatally, releasing his broken body only when she and her fellow tormentors deemed it time

she had read with horrified fascination.

She had looked at the reference in the book several times after that, wondering if a metal mistress was like an iron maiden, and if it was, why anyone would want to be anywhere around one.

Her curiosity had grown and grown, yet she had been reluctant to ask her mother about the mistress, half-afraid to know the answer. When her father had returned, the question had fairly tumbled out of her. He was shocked and puzzled by her query, until her mother, suddenly red-faced, had explained what Jaclyn had overheard. It was only years later that Jaclyn came to fully understand how a race car could surpass the love and desire men could experience for a human mistress.

There was a brief lull in the clamor of the pits. Jaclyn heard what sounded like Italian being spoken nearby. Her face brightened with anticipation as she scanned the area. There, just before that beautiful scarlet racer—wasn't that Gino Spinnelli? The man possessed the profile and the proud, arrogant stance of one of the statues she had seen in Rome, the dark olive of a skin kissed by the sun, and hair that fell in almost girlish curls on his forehead. He was speaking the Italian dialect in a rapid manner, gesturing expressively with long, strongly sculptured hands.

She assumed he was giving instructions about the car to the mechanic. It seemed so long since she had seen her friends or spoken the Italian they had taught her.

Jaclyn moved forward, hesitantly, straining for a better look, and then the man turned to face her. It *was* Gino! She caught his attention, then his curiosity. Suddenly recognition glinted in his brown eyes.

"Jaclyn, is that really you?" he cried in amazement, hurrying toward her, arms outstretched. She nodded, and he caught her up and swung her around exuberantly, holding her high in the air. When he finally set her down, still holding her firmly in the warm strength of his arms, her world spun. But she didn't want to see anything but his wide, white smile anyway. He was her connection with reality in this place that was now unreal and frightening.

She stared up into the tanned male face and saw familiar traces of the charming, impudent little boy she had played with when they were children. She hadn't seen him for four years, and time had added a mature handsomeness to the willful youth she had remembered. There, too, was the

13

caressing, possessive look that had always disconcerted her with its intensity.

"Come sta?" she pronounced carefully, and Gino nodded in approval.

"Benissimo, grazie. Da quanto tempo sei qui?"

"Wait a minute," she gasped at the flood of Italian. "That's about all I can recall, Gino!"

"Oh," he sighed. "I had hoped you'd remember how to speak my language. I am fine, thanks, Jaclyn. I asked how long you had been here?"

"I just arrived."

"I've missed you so," he whispered, lowering his face to hers, tightening his arms about her. "You have not forgotten the language of love, have you, *cara?*"

"No, Gino, not here!" she burst out.

He flung back his head, his eyes narrowing and his nostrils dilating in anger. "So, you no longer feel about Gino the way you did, eh?"

"No—I mean, yes—I—" she stammered. "Oh, let's talk about it later, please? I just got here, and there're so many people around, Gino. Where is Sophia?"

He stared at her, the corners of his mouth downturned, then just as suddenly as the look of pique had crossed his face it was gone, and he was smiling again. Jaclyn might have thought she imagined this other side of Gino, but she had experienced his quicksilver moods before.

"*Un momento,* Jaclyn, I will find her. We will, as you say, talk later."

Jaclyn breathed a sigh of relief as he left her to wind his way through the crowded pit area. She had been afraid Gino would behave this way. The relationship between them had become strained at their last meeting. She'd had

14

to confide tearfully to her father that Gino had become too persistent in his advances one night.

Her father had always been slow to anger, yet she had been surprised and a little apprehensive that she had told him about Gino. She had heard her parents arguing late that night, their voices hushed so that she couldn't hear properly, and her apprehension had grown.

There had been a scene the next day, right before the race, and everyone had looked on in bewildered disbelief as Gino and her father had argued out of earshot. Gino was the son of her father's best friend, and Jaclyn had often caught the hint that both families would like to see them married. The scene had become more and more tense until everyone was reminded that the starting time was getting close, and of necessity the two men had parted. Jaclyn's father had assured her he would explain everything later. But he never got to, for a few hours later he was dead.

"*Scusi, signorina,* would you please to stand over here?"

"What?" Jaclyn came out of her reverie. "Oh, sorry. I didn't mean to get in the way."

Moving to the place the man indicated, she watched as mechanics worked on the car, quickly making final preparations for the qualifying run she had come to see. The car was a dazzler, she thought, with its long, elegant lines, subdued power beneath the gleaming hood, and painted a glossy red. A red dark and rich like—blood, she thought. Shivering, she looked up, out onto the track, and watched another car race by.

Long moments passed, and Jaclyn gradually became aware of a strange prickling sensation at the back of her neck. Someone was watching her with an intensity she could feel. Curious, she looked around. To her right was stationed a silver car with a German driver and crew, to her left, a cobalt blue car. There didn't seem to be any driver in the blue car's space, and she wondered idly who it might be.

Caught in the motion of turning her head, her gaze was averted suddenly by a man standing in the shadows. A cobalt blue uniform hugged a body that hinted of strength and power, like the car he was standing beside. The breeze ruffled his hair, glinting blue-black in the sunlight.

At first she thought he was just leaning indolently against some boxes. But then she became aware of a power and tension about the man, like a coiled spring about to go off. His eyes were hidden by mirrored sunglasses, but she sensed that he saw, was aware of everything, even if she couldn't see behind those lenses that reflected the activity before him. She looked away with the self-consciousness of someone who is studied, like a butterfly on a pin, wondering if perhaps he watched her to screen out all the tension of the surroundings before he attempted to qualify.

It was hard to pretend a nonchalance she didn't feel, here in a place, a situation, where once she had felt so much at home. Now she felt strange, and even the casual glamor of an outfit intended to make her feel more confident and look a little older, more sophisticated for her work, seemed for nothing. As she felt his glance moving over the tailored cream blazer worn with a coffee-colored blouse, matching cream skirt, and calf-hugging boots, she remembered how Neil, her publisher, had told her such clothes only enhanced her femininity.

After a long, lingering appraisal that sent a blush skimming her cheekbones, his eyes returned to her face. She *knew* when they did, for she felt again that powerful awareness of him that she had felt minutes before. The subtlety of their awareness of each other in the midst of a crowded, noisy place was at once intimate, yet estranged. Here, in a place where no man looked at a beautiful woman in quite the same way as a beautiful automobile, it was a little unnerving for this to happen, she thought. And especially when she couldn't see behind his anonymous silver lenses.

Her attention was distracted by a scarlet flash at the periphery of her vision. A diminutive, scarlet-suited figure wearing a crash helmet approached her. Gloved hands reached to take off the protective headgear, and Jaclyn watched in surprise as a feminine face appeared. Dark, glossy curls spilled to the shoulders of the mannish uniform, which on closer inspection hinted at womanly curves beneath.

It was Sophia! she realized with a start. If she hadn't been preoccupied by the dark stranger's scrutiny, she would have guessed it sooner. The two ran to hug each other, Sophia pushing her helmet into her brother's hands as he came to stand beside her.

"It's been so long!" Sophia exclaimed when they had finally stood back and looked each other over.

"I can't believe it, even now," Jaclyn told her friend, gesturing at the scene around them. "Are you really going to co-drive with Gino in the race this weekend?"

Sophia nodded vigorously. Her brown eyes flashed with enthusiasm as she talked of the coming race. "I cannot believe it myself!" she admitted in her careful, accented English. "Gino has raced for many years, and I for only a few. Yet he has asked me to be his co-driver here!"

Gino shrugged. "It was time we raced together."

"At first I was not sure I wanted to participate in such a . . . a . . ." Sophia paused, searching for the proper word.

"Such an important and demanding race?" Gino offered helpfully, and his sister nodded her agreement.

"But tell me." Gino folded his arms across his chest and glared at her. "What do you mean by saying that I have raced for so many years, as you did a moment ago? Am I old and bent and gray? No, I am thirty, and that is not ancient, even if it is older than you, bambino!"

The two women laughed.

"Oh, Jaclyn, I am only bringing him down a bit. I suppose he has been trying to play Papa lately." She moved closer and slipped her arm into Gino's. "He knows that I am grateful for this chance."

"Daytona is a challenging race, and racecourse," Gino told Jaclyn, "and the only major twenty-four-hour event other than Le Mans. But here the race is run on a modern speedway instead of on country roads, as in France," he pointed out. "Sophia will learn much about herself as a driver here. This course will test her as few others could. And it will require all she can give in that twenty-four hours."

Jaclyn swung her glance around the course. The banks of the track rose steeply at the outer edges, and she had once heard a driver say it felt like being inside the rim of a teacup the first time he'd driven here. "Tell me what it feels like," she said.

"It's like . . . I'm flying," Sophia said, enthused. "Like a bird, almost, swooping down through the curves and down into the straightaways. *Fantastico!* And everyone here at the speedway has been so helpful. Because I am new here, not because I am a woman." There was a defensive note in her voice, and her face lost its animation.

"Sophia is feeling a little upset that some of the drivers are unsure about her ability," Gino explained to Jaclyn. "But I keep telling her that it is to be expected. She is a foreign driver here. They just don't know her ability yet."

"It is more than that with some of them!" Sophia interjected. "It is because I am a woman. Admit it!" She turned to Jaclyn. "I am not what you Americans call a women's libber. But I want to race. I have loved to drive from a very early age. It is a part of me, this urge. After all, is my name not Spinnelli? My uncle and my father and brother have all been race drivers—the best. It is in my blood."

Jaclyn listened to Sophia's impassioned plea for understanding. She'd known for years of her friend's burning desire to race, ever since they had played together in a dusty garage in Italy, as two men—one American and one Italian—worked with their crews on their latest race cars. Hadn't Sophia told Jaclyn that her mother had once been appalled to catch her happily teething on a wrench her father had offered Sophia while trying to work and babysit at the same time? He'd defended his actions to Sophia's indignant mother, saying that, after all, his tools were as clean as anything else his daughter gummed, but it had taken a long time before she had forgiven him. Knowing Mrs. Spinnelli's way of thinking, Jaclyn could well imagine that Sophia's father had been blamed somehow for Sophia's desire to race. Sophia had written that her mother had been the last of the family to accept her choice of career. Jaclyn remembered another time . . .

"What are you daydreaming about?" Gino broke in.

"I was thinking about the time your sister learned to drive by sitting on your father's lap. You were only five, Sophia, remember? I understand how you feel, Sophia, I really do. I wish you luck!" She held out a hand, and her friend grasped it, then they were hugging again, like two long-separated sisters. Which they had been, in a way, Jaclyn thought, fighting back happy tears at being reunited with both Gino and Sophia.

"Perhaps you can explain in the article you will write, eh, so that the readers will understand?" Sophia's question was hopeful.

Jaclyn nodded. "Of course."

They had to part then. It was nearly time for the Spinnellis to qualify their car for the race. As Jaclyn watched the two discuss their strategy, she marveled at the Italian woman's calm and her detached, professional manner. Sophia didn't show a trace of nervousness, or, worse, Jaclyn's father had once told her, the fevered urge to jump into the car, adrenaline racing beyond control in the veins. Sophia's concentration was total.

Gino could have taken the car for the qualifying run, but he had evidently decided to let Sophia do it. Perhaps, Jaclyn thought, Gino felt he could show the other drivers before the actual race that his sister had ability.

Jaclyn glanced over at the area next to the Spinnellis' space and saw that the man who had been watching her earlier was no longer standing in the shadows. Distracted by her friends, she had forgotten him. But she remembered him now, and the attraction she had sensed without words, with only a look. . . . Later she would ask Sophia or Gino the driver's name.

Sophia went through the complicated, careful preparations that were necessary before she could climb into the car. In addition to the fireproofed uniform, she wore protective shoes, and then pulled a sort of stocking cap over her head, called a balaclava. It covered her face and head, with holes cut out for her eyes. Over this she wore a helmet with her name proudly emblazoned in scarlet paint. A crew member performed the final act of readying her by taping on the protective gloves so that they wouldn't fly off in the event of a crash.

Once, Jaclyn had seen what happened to a driver who scorned gloves. Involved in a fiery crash, he had run from his car, screaming, toward the infield hospital, the skin hanging in scorched shreds from his hands. He never raced without gloves after that.

"You see how safe we are trying to make the sport."

Jaclyn turned at the sound of the softly spoken words and found that Gino had come to stand at her side. She found that she had stiffened with apprehension while she watched her friend. At Gino's warm, understanding smile, she relaxed and smiled back.

"But if they make it too safe, you wouldn't want to race, would you?" she asked lightly.

Gino chuckled. "Probably not. Didn't someone once say that life is sweetened by risk?"

Now Sophia was getting into the car and fastening her safety harness. Gino left Jaclyn to stride over and give his sister a good-luck kiss, albeit through a helmet.

Then it was time. The engine flared to life as the crew stepped away. Jaclyn wondered if this scarlet machine liked a feminine hand at the wheel, and if racing was for Sophia the all-consuming passion that it was for many men. Did the deep rumbling of that engine assume more importance for her than the beating of a man's heart?

Later there would be time to ask her friend that and so many other questions the magazine readers, and she, too, would want answered about this woman. She knew that some people would be surprised at Sophia. There were still those who expected that a woman who invaded a male's

21

terrain would look and act mannish. As feminine and attractive as any woman, Sophia was very different from that stereotype, yet deeply interested in a sport that remained predominantly masculine.

Remembering that she had to write the article, Jaclyn pulled a notepad and pencil out of her bag and began making brief notes. Glancing up, she saw that Sophia was looking in her direction. She watched as Sophia's gloved hands left the steering wheel, raised to form a familiar signal. Jaclyn felt the color drain from her face, saw the whole scene dissolve into a colorful blur as her eyes filled with tears.

Now that Sophia held her hands in that manner, apparently remembering, slowly Jaclyn raised hers and saluted in the old way, as they had when they were children. Sophia nodded energetically, her expression hidden behind the face shield of the helmet and the balaclava. Then her car was gone, accelerating down pit road.

She guided the car out onto the track, around the steeply banked turns, swiftly, surely, through the turns and then the straightaway, again and again.

Gino was timing the run with a stopwatch, and by the satisfied look on his face Jaclyn could tell Sophia was doing well. Of course, with the reputation he had for winning, he was offered only the best his sponsoring car manufacturer could provide. Thus Sophia could not have had a better chance for her American debut.

"Golly, are you one of those media ladies?"

Startled by the familiar, teasing voice, Jaclyn looked up. "Well, if it isn't Scott Green, the boy wonder of the photography department. I thought you were sent down yesterday."

He frowned. "You didn't see me a minute ago? I was

standing over there," he said, gesturing to a spot only a few yards away. "You're always saying you can see me in a crowd, with this hair of mine. And you looked right in my direction. Is something wrong, Jaclyn?"

"No, why?"

"I dunno. You seem kinda tense, distracted or something. You didn't see me when you looked right in my direction a little while ago. And just before I came over here you looked downright upset, before you held your hands up. What was that you did to Miss Spinnelli?"

"Just—a signal for good luck, that's all," she said, shrugging. "Wait, I want to see how she does through this turn."

"Oh. I thought it might be kinda special." Scott didn't notice her attempt to change the subject. "I got a shot of it."

"No, Scott, you didn't!"

"Hey, it's no big deal. I'm not going to give it to anyone but you. I heard that you and the boss argued over playing up your friendship with the Spinnellis in the magazine article."

"I'm sorry, Scott. I didn't mean to sound so sharp." She stared up at him, her expression troubled. "I'm a little tense, I guess."

His thin shoulders jerked up and then down in a shrug. "No sweat. But what's bothering you? You don't look like you're enjoying yourself much. I thought— Hey, I gotta run, she's about to come in."

Scott, too, had noticed Jaclyn's tenseness. She watched Sophia's car make the final timed round of the course, and wondered if coming here had been wise. Memories were being awakened, and not just pleasant ones. . . .

The car entered pit road, and then Sophia was braking

to a stop before the pit space. Jaclyn watched while everyone seemed to come to attention when the speed was announced over the speedway loudspeaker. Then a cheer went up, both in the pits—by Gino and a jubilant crew—and by a crowd of obvious Spinnelli fans who had attended the qualifying.

Sophia was mobbed by a happy group of mechanics when she emerged from the car, and she spent several minutes trying to extricate herself so that she could remove her headgear and gloves. Applause greeted Gino's proud, brotherly kiss and hug, and a group of reporters and photographers gathered around. Successful women race drivers were still such a rarity that Sophia's being there and doing well rated a bit more attention for the moment from the press than other drivers.

Indeed, Jaclyn had had no trouble selling the editor of her favorite magazine, *Life-Styles,* on an article about Sophia. The editor had arranged to feature it in the next issue. It would mean a tight deadline, but the opportunity to meet up with old friends had been too good to pass up.

"How did I do?" Sophia, her eyes still sparkling with excitement, wanted to know when she broke free of the press. Jaclyn had stayed at the back of the pit space, knowing that her friend would give her all the time she could for questions back at the hotel where they were all to stay.

"Marvelously!" Jaclyn complimented, hugging her. "You'll do the Spinnelli name proud."

"Ah, but let's not get overconfident," Gino admonished. Sophia grew sober under his brotherly rebuke. Then Gino's face creased into a wide grin, and he laughed. "Relax, *bambino,* I am just teasing you. Tonight, I think we must have a celebration, eh?"

"Yes!" Sophia beamed, obviously relieved that Gino hadn't been serious. Then she looked up at him through long black lashes, a mischievous expression on her face.

"Did you notice my fans, Gino?" she asked, her red lips curving into an impish smile. "Tell me, brother, if our pit area is decorated with flowers as yours was in that last race, how will you know if they are for you or for me?"

The two women laughed as Gino reddened. Everyone knew that Gino's reputation with the fans was not just because he raced with such daring, but because of his brown-eyed Italian charm as well.

Neil Farrell had asked that Jaclyn bring back an interview with Gino as well as the one with Sophia. Always make the most of an opportunity was his motto, he'd said. Frequently. In the beginning of their working relationship Neil had had trouble understanding why Jaclyn preferred her middle name to the familiar one of her famous father. She'd wanted to make it on her own, not on the coattails of someone else's fame, she'd responded, and matters had seemed smooth until this interview had come up, and with it Neil's urging that Jaclyn play up her past relationship with the Spinnellis, her personal background, in the story and pictures. She'd begun to wonder if she shouldn't make a change from writing mainly for Neil's magazine.

Which reminded Jaclyn that she was supposed to be working. She sighed. "Well, now would be a good time to get some reaction to your run from the other drivers, Sophia. I can see a group of them over there, and they must be discussing you, because one man keeps looking over here. He doesn't look very happy."

Sophia glanced over in the direction Jaclyn had indicated with a slight motion of her head. She smiled, but there was a bitter twist to her lips.

"That one is Signor Forrest, the one who has been most critical of me to the press," she told Jaclyn.

"Then I had better go talk to him," Jaclyn said with a smile. She reached into her purse to switch on a portable tape recorder.

"Why do you use that machine?" Gino wanted to know.

"It helps me keep things straight. And I don't have to worry later if someone says I've misquoted them." Too often she'd heard people claim that they hadn't said what appeared in print. She had vowed it wouldn't happen to her, and she had the tapes to back her up, so her growing reputation as a fair and honest interviewer had remained unsullied. The tapes helped also when she wasn't able to take notes as precisely as she wanted to.

After promising to meet the Spinnellis for the ride to the hotel, Jaclyn set off in the direction of the drivers. When she had first heard that Gino and Sophia were coming to this country, she'd written to Sophia, thinking she might do an article about her while they renewed their friendship. But there was another reason, too, why Jaclyn had wanted to go there. Four years was long enough, she'd told herself, to hide from something that had been as much a part of her life as racing had been once. She had to face old ghosts, make peace with her past. She had to prove to herself that a scene such as this could be faced again.

It hadn't been too hard so far, really, she reflected, raising her face to the sun as she walked. And after she finished the article she would have a few days to lie on the beach and soak up some sun before she went back home to the apartment she shared with her mother. It had been so cold in New York when she'd left earlier that day.

As Jaclyn approached the drivers she assumed a confident look, trying to hide the nervousness she felt at having so many men looking at her. Actually she would have liked to believe that they appreciated her looks. Any woman would. But she knew that if any car had been on the course then, no mere woman would have received their attention or their curiosity. Plainly they were curious about her presence there. Looking down, Jaclyn realized that her press badge was missing. Well, too late now, she thought. They'll know soon enough who I am and why I'm here.

Most drivers were accustomed to publicity, she knew, recognizing it as a part—a necessary and sometimes enjoyable part—of the whole racing activity. What did it matter, most reasoned, how well a driver did at a race if no one but those who had attended knew the outcome? And having a name well known to the public always helped when a driver was trying to find a sponsor. Jaclyn identified herself and asked for their comments on Sophia's entrance in the race. What was their reaction to Sophia? she wanted to know.

Several spoke up, all saying that they thought she had done well. No, they didn't mind racing with a woman, most said. Where, Jaclyn wondered, had Sophia gotten the idea that they were against her entering the race? After all, these men rarely minced words.

"Well, I don't like it, don't like it at all," a stocky man growled, and Jaclyn recognized him as the man Sophia had pointed out as her chief antagonist. He jabbed at the air with an expensive cigar as he spoke, blasting Sophia for "trying to be better than a man. I suppose," he continued, "that she's trying to prove that a woman can do anything. Who needs their skirts flapping in the breeze? Next thing

27

you know they'll be in our pit crews, fixing their makeup instead of the engines just before a race."

There was subdued, uncomfortable laughter. Jaclyn knew that the men were watching her for a reaction to the comment about her sex, but she was too professional to show how she felt.

One man tried to gloss over the lull in the conversation by teasing Forrest for never having forgiven the woman racer of years past who had painted her car pink, and who had, in fact, even dyed her hair pink.

"Well, what's this one trying to prove, anyway?" Forrest wanted to know.

"Perhaps she's trying to prove something to herself, not to the rest of us," someone said.

The group parted to let the owner of the deep, somewhat familiar voice come forward. Jaclyn knew her jaw dropped in surprise as a tall man dressed in a cobalt blue uniform stepped into the circle. Now, without the sunglasses, she knew the identity of the man who had stood in the shadows of the pits and had watched her, sending out that wave of attraction she had felt across all the frenetic activity of the place.

It was Shane Jaeger, the actor who raced as a "hobby" and was more elusive than Garbo from the curious, prying eyes of the public. He was warmly welcomed into the group, seemingly a well-liked member of the closely knit racing kinship. But the indignant driver interrupted the friendly greetings.

"What do you mean?" he asked. "What does she have to prove to herself?" He stood, hands on hips in an aggressive posture, obviously not happy that he had been interrupted, or, more likely, upstaged by the popular Jaeger.

"I mean that she might be trying to prove to herself that

28

she has the ability to be as good as anyone," Jaeger told him. "Growing up in a family such as hers, she probably picked up the desire to race at an early age. It's very natural to her. I haven't heard her claiming to be here for any reason other than to try to be an international racer such as her brother. She's said to be very knowledgeable in this sport. And quite charming when you meet her, I've heard."

"Charming? Big deal!" the man scoffed, apparently not appeased.

"Well, you must admit that with her background she is a better rookie than most are at the beginning," Jaeger calmly returned. "Besides, just how long did we men think we could keep all this to ourselves?"

Jaeger's easy, deferential manner seemed to bring Forrest around more than his actual words. The driver's face had lost its angry expression as he listened to Jaeger.

"But still"—gray bursts of cigarette smoke erupted from the man's mouth, making him resemble a dragon— "still, I'm going to be watching out for her this weekend. After all, you can't trust a rookie," he muttered darkly.

Jaeger threw his head back and laughed, the deep, rumbling sound of a man thoroughly enjoying himself. But it was obviously a private joke, because the others didn't laugh, and the driver who had been somewhat mollified now stiffened and demanded to know what was so funny.

"Don't you remember?" the actor asked, trying to still his chuckles.

"No, what?"

Amusement lurked in eyes, which were a brilliant silver-gray in the sunlight, eyes that were surrounded by tiny laugh lines. Here, Jaclyn thought, was a man who looked like he enjoyed life.

"You," he pointed with a long, accusing finger, "used those very words about me several years ago when I began racing."

"Eh?" The man looked at Jaeger, his expression wary.

"As a matter of fact," he went on, "you said you'd be watching out for that 'darned rookie,' calling me an 'actor type who thinks this is a kiddie race,' remember?"

There was an uneasy silence as the driver stared at Jaeger, and a dull red flush spread up his face. But then, as he realized that Jaeger bore no grudge and he even found the memory of those words funny, he laughed.

"Made your point, Shane," he replied jovially, and he slapped the younger man on the back. "And some driver that rookie turned out to be, too." His compliment was gruff but sincere.

Was that why the man had defended Sophia? Jaclyn wondered. At first Jaclyn had thought that Jaeger had said what he did because he felt Sophia was a sort of underdog, being the only woman entered in the race. But he seemed to be defending Sophia because of her rookie status there, as he would any driver, whatever sex. Sophia would be pleased, Jaclyn reflected. That was how she wanted it—no special favors bestowed upon her because she was a woman, but no restrictions or opposition because of it, either.

Jaeger turned to listen to a man who had approached him. Dressed in faded jeans, a dilapidated jacket, and a Stetson, the man seemed a little out of place among the younger, international grouping of men whose occupation and dress made them seem glamorous.

While Jaeger and the man conferred, some of the other drivers drifted away, and Jaclyn decided it was time to walk back to the Spinnelli area. She toyed for a moment with the idea of asking the actor a few questions. She knew of his aversion to the press, but he had joined the group while she stood talking with the others. Didn't that mean it would be okay, that he knew what she was and accepted her?

But then she looked down at her notepad and realized that she had written little on it, and nothing since Jaeger had joined the group. Her press badge was missing, and he hadn't been near when she had introduced herself. She bit her lip and frowned, trying to decide what to do. Since he avoided the press, not much was known about the actor. The mystique had proved to have an opposite effect on press and public alike. Instead of being left alone, he had been pursued. Some people criticized his attempts to remain a private person, saying that he owed his public something offscreen as well as on.

The wind ruffled his hair, a deep, rich black. Chiseled features—almost too angular cheekbones, a long, straight nose, a firm yet sensuous mouth, and a lean jaw—combined to make a distinctive-looking face that commanded attention. His wasn't the face of Hollywood's standard handsome leading man. But he had a magnetism, a presence, that couldn't be ignored, on screen or off. The power of his gray eyes, which changed color with his moods, was mesmerizing as he turned to look at Jaclyn and she found them boring into her like steely silver nails.

Even while he listened to the man, Jaeger's glance locked with Jaclyn's. He moved toward her, started to speak, then frowned and stopped as the man who had approached him before followed him. All of a sudden Jaclyn knew she couldn't ask Jaeger any questions or even talk to him then. Something about the mutual message of attraction, flashed without words almost as if they stood

31

alone, had left her shaken. She slipped away and walked quickly back to the Spinnelli pit area.

She had been surprised when Jaeger had popped up like that. Yet she remembered from her research that this was a race he frequently entered.

Gino was not yet ready to leave. "It's Jaeger's turn soon," he told her. "I want to see how his car does. I intend to beat him this year."

Was there some rivalry between the men? Jaclyn asked herself. She knew that Jaeger had finished the race better than Gino last year, but she sensed that there was more to the story than that. But now was not the time to ask, as Gino was intently watching the activities in Jaeger's pit space with a concentration he hadn't given any other driver or car. The jetlike whine of another car making the rounds of the course echoed around them, and then all was silent as it came time for Jaeger to qualify.

At his crew's signal that all was ready, he stopped the pacing he'd been doing to relieve tension and slid into his car. His face became anonymous inside the glassy shadows of the visored helmet and the car windshield. Now the man became just another driver who merged with his machine. His touch brought the engine to pulsating life. After assuring himself that the engine revved properly and all was right, he gave a confident, thumbs-up signal to his crew and drove down and out of the pits.

Guided by Jaeger's expert handling, the car moved around the speedway as if it were one with the sinuously curving surface. Gino shook his head and muttered in Italian to himself as he kept an eye on his stopwatch.

"It looks as if I'm going to have trouble with him again this year," he told her.

Jaclyn continued to watch as Jaeger's car finished the

32

timed laps. Suddenly chunks of rubber flew up from one wheel, and the car spun wildly out of control, swerving and coming within inches of the retaining wall. The crowd seemed to hold its breath collectively as Jaeger regained control and finally brought his wayward machine to a harmless halt on the grassy verge beside the paved course.

Then he was out of the car and signaling to the track officials that he was unharmed. His crew jumped the low pit wall and raced toward the disabled car. Jaeger had pulled off his headgear and was now calmly assessing the damage, which was apparently not serious. He appeared as unconcerned about the accident as if he had merely had a flat while out on a Sunday drive, instead of blowing a tire while blazing a scorching path around a curving, challenging racecourse at speeds several times that allowed on the highway.

Everyone had recovered from the surprise of the incident, and they were now exchanging comments about the way Jaeger had handled the car. Jaclyn let out her breath and silently admired the man for his skillful driving. It had been a long time since she had seen someone handle a car the way he had.

"I wondered if he'd have a problem with those new tires his sponsor wanted him to try," she overheard Gino saying to a mechanic, with a note of—satisfaction? No, it couldn't be, she chided herself. He turned to her. "Ready?"

"Yes, but what about Sophia?"

She was in a conference with speedway officials and veteran drivers, he informed Jaclyn, to instruct her and other rookie drivers on important handling tips about the course. She would return to the hotel later.

As Jaclyn and Gino walked through the pit area, she

saw that many curious eyes followed them. She knew that many people, fans and crews alike, were speculating about her being Gino's latest conquest. She slanted a glance at him, asking herself if she had the nerve to find out if he had brought anyone here with him to watch him compete.

Gino's arm slid possessively around her shoulders. Startled, she wondered why he was suddenly adopting such a familiar manner with her, and was about to ask when she saw Shane Jaeger striding toward them on his way to his pit space.

"Gino," Jaeger acknowledged with a slight nod of his dark head.

"*Buon giorno,* Shane," Gino said quietly. He threw his head back, chin thrust forward, his stance cocky and confident. Only Jaclyn knew the tension that corded the muscles of the arm encircling her.

The two men stood staring at each other, and animosity hung between them, tangible as the pungent fumes of fuel and the raucous noises of people and machines. Then Jaeger's eyes moved toward Jaclyn in an inquiring movement, and Gino was forced to introduce them.

Her fingers tingled after contact with his strong, warm clasp, but his eyes were as cold and hard as metal as he silently made note of Gino's possessive arm. She hadn't wanted it around her, but she could hardly ask Gino to remove it under the watchful eyes of his rival.

"It's nice to meet you, Miss Taylor," he said. He looked again at Gino. "I was hoping to meet your sister," he told him, and Gino coolly informed him that Sophia had stayed behind for a meeting.

"But we're having a celebration party later, and we'll all be there," Gino added, sliding an oblique look in Jaclyn's

34

direction, implying that she would be with him. "Would you like to come?"

Jaeger's mouth quirked into an ironic smile as the two men assessed each other, then his glance slid to Jaclyn for a long moment. "Perhaps," he said shortly. With a curt nod, he left them.

"Was that necessary?" Jaclyn asked as soon as Jaeger was out of earshot. Slipping out from under Gino's arm, she turned to face him, her eyes sparkling with anger.

"What?" Gino asked innocently.

"Why were you trying to give him the impression that I'm your—your property or something?" she accused.

"Jaclyn, Jaclyn," he chided, looking injured. "I was just trying to protect you from him, that's all. He's got quite a reputation for loving and leaving beautiful women like you."

She laughed, a clear, high peal of merriment, which caused heads to turn in curiosity.

Gino frowned. "What's so funny?" he demanded.

"Oh, I can't help it," she gasped, trying to stop. "That's the funniest thing I've ever heard, Gino. Really, that's like the wolf trying to save the lamb from—from—" She broke off, searching for the proper word.

He stiffened. "I am not a wolf. Just because I appreciate women, I gain an underserved reputation for being a womanizer, eh?"

"Oh, Gino." Jaclyn sighed and shook her head in friendly disbelief. "I'll bet you loved every minute of gaining and maintaining that reputation. You were a charmer even when you were a little boy. And did you ever think about the possibility that Jaeger might not deserve the reputation he's got either?"

He shrugged but didn't look convinced. They walked on

to his elegant, expensive rental car. "I can't be blamed for not wanting to compete with him once more." He opened her car door with a flourish and helped her inside. "We both found the same woman desirable once before," he said softly as he rested his arms on the upper edge of the door and stared down at her, his eyes dark with desire. "It appears that we do once again."

Her eyes widened in surprise. She couldn't quite believe her ears. Gino found her desirable, when he'd known her since childhood, when she'd deliberately spurned contact with him for the last four years? Surprising.

But Jaeger? That someone else had noticed that he was attracted to her seemed to make it even more real. How disturbing.

She turned to look out at the speedway as Gino started the car. It had been an emotional day full of renewed friendship, anticipation, excitement, discovery. And memories, haunting memories that had kept her from a place such as this for four years. Would she be sorry that she had come?

CHAPTER TWO

Jaclyn stood before the mirror and surveyed her appearance with satisfaction. She wore an unusual outfit, at least for her, and one she doubted many other women would be wearing that night. The sleek lines of it flattered her figure, and the sea-green shade intensified the color of her eyes. The style made it special. It was a jumpsuit, styled after those worn by race drivers and mechanics.

But on her it looked entirely feminine, as some male-styled garments did on women. This brought her delicate blond beauty into prominence as much or more than any drifting chiffon creation might. Styled with slightly wide, flaring legs, the jumpsuit had details on the collar and pockets, outlined with gold thread, and was worn with a gold belt. She had found the outfit in a boutique back home, and liked the way it made her feel—young and alive, and free of any associations the style of clothing might have.

Sitting in front of the mirror, Jaclyn brushed out her center-parted hair, which fell simply to her shoulders, and thought about the party she'd be attending that night.

Never had she thought she'd be celebrating her friend's entrance in a race, even though she had known since childhood about Sophia's desire to become a race driver.

What different paths their lives had taken as adults, when at one time their backgrounds had been so alike.

Searching in a small jewelry case for the tiny gold hoop earrings she planned to wear, her fingers brought out something she hadn't worn or looked at for a long time, yet had always carried with her. It was a gold charm bracelet that had been a gift for her eighteenth birthday four years ago. She remembered what it looked like without having gazed at it all this time. She held it up to the lamp, and the light reflected off the tiny gold charms that dangled from a delicate link bracelet, sending tiny shafts of brilliance off the diamond and emerald chips that decorated certain charms.

Each charm had some special significance for her. A typewriter with golden keys represented her love of writing. Several were reminders of places the three of them—her mother and father and herself, an only child—had visited when her father was alive. A golden shell brought back the memory of a beach on the vividly blue Mediterranean where they had first met the Spinnellis. Now she was here, renewing that friendship, near a Florida beach. Jaclyn finally came to the last charm that had been added, to be worn only once.

It was a tiny, exquisitely crafted race car. An emerald-helmeted driver sat behind the wheel, and diamond chips outlined the number eighteen on the car door. She fastened the bracelet on her wrist and touched the tiny car with trembling fingers. A slight motion of her wrist set the charms into motion. The gentle tinkling sound was familiar, somehow reassuring. She remembered the love that had gone into each charm's selection by her parents, especially that little car. Perhaps it *was* time to wear it again.

People had often told her that she resembled her mother, a slender blonde with a gentle look about her. But she could see traces of her father in the pensive emerald-green eyes that stared back at her from the mirror. Her mother often teased Jaclyn that she most resembled her father when she got a glint of determination in those eyes and tilted her chin stubbornly, and she had always to laugh and agree. She could remember that look of his, too.

The two of them had been drawn closer together after his death. Her mother called Jaclyn a "legacy of love" from her husband. Somehow the two of them held each other up during bad moments.

Jaclyn had grown up quickly since her father's death. With her growing maturity she felt the need to find a career, and it was by chance that a friend of her mother's saw some of Jaclyn's work one day. She helped launch Jaclyn into magazine writing by arranging for an interview with an editor.

The editor had told Jaclyn that she had a flair for understanding and writing about people, and she found she loved interviewing so much that she never wrote anything but profiles after that. She had been successful, far beyond her wildest dreams, but her head hadn't been turned by her success. A small book, a collection of some of her better interviews, had been published recently. She thought of herself as the interviewer of interesting people, a writer who brought them to print so that they could be read about and appreciated for their special gift of living life to the fullest, whether they were famous or just supposedly "ordinary people." But the success of her book had guaranteed that she could work free-lance and contribute to only those magazines she wished to, and thus be her own boss. It was a relief to feel she wasn't so dependent on sales from a magazine owned by Neil Farrell, who had been pressuring her lately about writing the Spinnelli piece in a way she didn't want to.

Jaclyn left her room and made her way upstairs to the rooftop restaurant, where the party was already in full swing. Accepting a glass of champagne from a passing waiter, she went to stand near the huge window overlooking the ocean and gaze longingly at the wide, pale-sanded beach below her.

Dusk was falling. Lights from homes and hotels were beginning to twinkle up and down the shoreline, making a jeweled necklace of varied colors that sparkled, reflecting off the dark, silken waves. She longed to be outside, breathing in the sea breezes that had teased her senses earlier when Gino had driven them to the hotel. There hadn't been time for anything but a tantalizing glimpse of the ocean. But she was determined to spend more time on the beach during the next few days when she wasn't busy with Sophia, and after the race when she'd finished the article in her hotel room.

Belatedly remembering why she was there, she turned to look for Sophia but couldn't find her. As she turned back to the window, Jaclyn caught a glimpse of someone out of the corner of her eye, and looked back in disbelief. Shane Jaeger was entering the room. She was even more surprised to see him at the party than she had been earlier at the speedway, for he was known to scorn the party scene.

Others had noticed his appearance, too, but he had such an unapproachable air about him that he was left alone. Finally, apparently not finding the person he sought, he walked to the bar and ordered a drink. He was dressed casually in a black turtleneck shirt and formfitting slacks, with a tan suede sport jacket. There was an easy yet expensive elegance about the way he wore his clothes that out-classed the more formally dressed men in the room.

Someone touched Jaclyn's elbow, and she jumped, near-ly spilling her champagne. It was Gino. He looked very Italian and good-looking in a gray dress suit and stark white shirt, which played up the darkness of his hair and olive skin.

"*Cara,* you look lovely tonight," he complimented her. "Now, if Signor Forrest could see you dressed like this, I think he would change his mind about women in the pit areas."

She laughed at his reference to the driver who had been dubious of Sophia and other women race drivers earlier that day. "Where is your sister?" she asked.

"We'll find her later," he said in a low, caressing voice. "We have to make up for lost time, you and I, eh?"

But even as she tried to concentrate on his potent charm, she was aware of Shane Jaeger in the room. As her eyes wandered from Gino's face again he mistook her lack of attention and searching eyes for her being anxious to find Sophia. Grudgingly he led her over to where his sister stood talking with a man. Sophia looked like a fashion model in a black, off-one-shoulder tunic and matching skirt, and for a moment Jaclyn could imagine her to be one, until Jaclyn moved closer and found Sophia to be arguing the merits of one engine versus another with a silver-haired, slightly stooped man.

Jaclyn wondered why the man looked familiar, then knew for certain as the man looked up and watched her and Gino approach.

"Giuseppe!" she cried, and flung herself into the arms of the man who had been like a favorite uncle to her when she was a child. She was hugged affectionately, and then

41

Giuseppe held her at arm's length so that he could look her over.

"I am touched that you remember me," he told her with a gentle smile. "You have grown into a beautiful young woman. It is a wonder that the skinny little thing with blond pigtails has grown into someone so lovely, is it not, Gino?"

"Well, when I saw her last, she had long since given up the pigtails, but I know what you mean." Gino laughed.

"Giuseppe retired years ago when my father did, but we persuaded him to come here with us," Sophia explained.

The four of them reminisced about what Giuseppe called "the good old days," the time when they had first known each other. Jaclyn looked up once and found the eyes of several partygoers on their group, apparently wondering what she, a blond American, was doing chatting away as if she were one of the group of dark Italians. Jaclyn was a part of them, and yet not, but for a brief time it seemed as if the years had melted away and she belonged again.

Their talk touched on many topics, mostly racing, but when Gino joked about the near crash he had been involved in the previous month, and proudly showed off the scar he'd been left with, Jaclyn's smile froze on her face. The gaiety went out of the party for her as she suddenly remembered why she had felt so strange here among these people, friendly though they were. She found herself mumbling something about getting some fresh air, and was aware that Sophia laid a hand on her brother's arm to stop him as he started to follow. As Jaclyn moved through the crowded room she saw a balcony outside the sliding glass doors ahead of her.

She slid the doors open and stepped outside. Cool sea

breezes fanned her flushed face as she closed the doors behind her and walked over to lean her elbows on the decorative railing that bordered the balcony. She watched the rolling waves below her and felt a measure of calm returning. Two lovers strolled along the shoreline of the moonlit ocean, their arms linked. They stopped for an occasional kiss, oblivious to the water swirling around their feet, even to the onlooking Jaclyn.

The breeze feathered through Jaclyn's hair, gently lifting it away from her face in moon-silvered strands. She sighed at the thought of having to return to the party inside.

Someone opened the glass doors, and for a moment the sounds of the party burst out raucously on her solitude until they were shut. She found herself bracing for Gino's intrusion, and turned to meet him. A tall, obviously male figure stood in the shadows of the balcony. But the man was too tall to be Gino.

"I'm sorry if I've disturbed you." The vibrant, attractive voice belonged to Shane Jaeger.

"You—you haven't," she stammered. She turned back to lean on the railing, feeling a little in need of support as the man moved to her side and rested his elbows on the metal.

Unlike Gino, he seemed to have no need to compliment her excessively or flirt, but stood as she did, quietly savoring the beauty and peace of the ocean. After several minutes had passed she glanced at him. He looked as unapproachable as he had earlier when he had entered the party room. She wondered if he had found the person he had been seeking, and was startled when he turned and looked at her.

"Are you feeling better?" he asked.

"Better?" She frowned, confused.

"You looked upset as you walked out here a few minutes ago."

"Oh, that." She understood now what he was asking. He had seen her with the Spinnellis, watched her abrupt departure from the room. Was that why he had come out? she asked herself. She nervously traced a swirl on the railing as she tried to think of what to say.

"Perhaps it concerns Gino and isn't any of my business."

"No, it wasn't anything like that," she said quickly. "It really wasn't anything important." She didn't know how to tell him what had upset her. She couldn't explain it without dragging up the past, and she shied away from doing that. Only a few people knew, and she wasn't sure they really understood. She couldn't expect him to be any different.

Why did he bother talking to her, anyway, when she was a member of the press he so despised? she asked herself. Could it be that he didn't know? She remembered he had walked up to the group at the speedway after she had introduced herself. But she'd had her pen and notepad in her hand. Not that she remembered to use them after the surprise of his joining the group. Should she tell him?

"It's beautiful out here tonight, isn't it?" Jaclyn heard him saying while she worried about what to do.

She nodded in agreement. "I hadn't really expected it to be this warm here in February."

"Where are you from?" he wanted to know.

She told him and he nodded. "It *is* warm here compared to New York," he agreed with a smile. "It's my favorite time of year here."

"You sound as if you come here often."

44

"I live here."

"Here?" Surprised, her voice came out a little louder than normal.

"Shhh," he cautioned. "There might be one of those nosy press people around."

She stiffened, unsure if he was teasing or being serious.

"Why shouldn't I?" he was saying. "An actor doesn't have to live in Hollywood. I can commute, and this place suits me between films and races." He loved the city, he told her.

"You know, it surprised me that you could drive on the beach," she remarked.

He nodded. "At first I thought it strange to see a sign on the beach, marking a place where a land speed record was set, when drivers today are limited to ten miles per hour for the beachgoers' safety. Did you know that this was one of the first speed capitals of the world?"

She shook her head, and he went on to tell her how Sir Malcolm Campbell of the United Kingdom had set a land speed record of 276 miles per hour along that beach, how eleven speed records had been set on it, and that Daytona Beach and its sister city to the north, Ormond Beach, had recently celebrated more than eighty years of automobile racing.

He told her the history of the area, beginning in 1902 when someone interested the Ormond Hotel in sponsoring beach races. The hotel, an imposing, elegant queen, still stood overlooking the Halifax River, not far from the beach. The wealthy gathered there in the old days to escape the harsh chill of the north, and after that year, there was a new sport to occupy them. From then on the beach was the scene of cars of every description, size, and purpose.

First had come the cumbersome-looking, hand-built cars with fragile-looking spoke wheels. Then long, sleek cars that were out to break speed records. Next were the stockers, cars fresh from the assembly line, looking much like those on the road but with adjustments to the engines, which made their speed much greater on the racetrack. And finally modern cars that cruised the length of the beach only for the enjoyment of their drivers and passengers.

Those daring men of long ago had broken one speed record after another, until finally more space was needed, and the car manufacturers and drivers had moved on to the Bonneville Salt Flats in Utah, Jaeger told Jaclyn.

He hesitated then and laughed a little self-consciously. "Now I'm sounding like Mitch."

"Who's he?"

"Mitch Corbin, a friend of mine," he explained. "He's a former race driver who lives here. A bit of a character, Mitch is. Now that he's retired he's become an authority on the local racing history, and he helps run a museum of racing memorabilia."

Jaclyn smiled. "He must be a fascinating person to know. Tell me more."

"Well, before the speedway was built, the stock cars raced a course along the beach and a parallel street. Those were Mitch's favorite days. There weren't many rules, and sometimes the drivers used that to their advantage. One fellow, Mitch told me, had a cohort jump into his car with a can of gasoline, so that he could skip a pit stop. The officials made sure that sort of thing was illegal, after that."

It was plain to Jaclyn, as Jaeger talked, that it was a different era that fascinated him, the days when rakish millionaires raced on the eve of the automotive age, days of cars called Golden Arrow, Pirate, and Bullet, racing at speeds recorded at an unheard of fifty-seven miles per hour. A time when it was often likely that a driver and his machine would be pulled from the salty waters of the Atlantic when his car veered out of control.

Some years back Ormond Beach had begun the beach races again, he told her, with spectators sitting on the dunes to watch vintage cars with modern-day drivers.

"You seem to have more than a casual interest in racing," Jaeger said suddenly.

"Yes, I guess you could say that."

"Is that how you know the Spinnellis?"

"Their family and mine have been friends for a long time," she said carefully.

"I thought there might be a closer relationship than that." He turned to look at her. "With Gino, I mean."

She shook her head. "I think of Gino as a brother," she said in a light voice.

"Then the impression I got this afternoon was erroneous?"

She nodded, smiling wryly. "I don't know why Gino did that. I guess he thought that, that—" She floundered.

"That I'd get the idea that it was hands-off?" His forehead creased into a frown, and he muttered something about "carrying a grudge."

"What?" Jaclyn asked.

"Nothing. Tell me about yourself."

Jaclyn wondered if she should find out now if he knew that she was a journalist. Somehow, although they had just talked for a short time, they communicated in a way she'd never experienced with a man. She was a little afraid that it all might change if he knew, that is, if he didn't

47

already know. Not that she was ashamed of what she did. Far from it. But if it was going to matter, better to get it over with now, she decided.

"Mr. Jaeger?" she began, but he interrupted, inviting her to call him Shane, if he could call her Jaclyn. "Of course." She smiled. "But I have something I should tell you about myself." She was disconcerted by his soft laughter.

"Some deep, dark secret, with your innocent looks?" he asked, amused.

She frowned and searched his face for some sign of sarcasm. But there was none. "Please, I'm serious."

"Okay, I'm sorry. Go on." He was attempting to control the twitching at the corners of his mouth. "I know you're Jaclyn Taylor," he said when she told him her name again. "And you've told me I can call you Jaclyn."

"If you don't call me something worse," she muttered.

"What?"

"Nothing," she said heavily. "I mean—yes, you may call me Jaclyn. But after what I tell you, maybe you won't want to speak to me at all. You see, I—" Her words were interrupted by a loud sliding open and shutting of the glass doors.

"Conducting a little secret interview out here, you two?" Gino rasped angrily, insinuation in his voice.

Jaclyn grimaced and silently wished he hadn't picked that moment to interrupt them. She managed a smile and apologized for staying outside for so long, saying she hoped he hadn't been looking for her. But Gino wasn't mollified. He took a gulp of his drink and moved rather unsteadily toward them. Jaclyn had the awful feeling that he was spoiling for a scene.

"I looked all over for you, Jaclyn, thinking you were

upset. But you were out here all this time with *him*. *Interviewing* the famous Shane Jaeger, I suppose," he sneered.

"Please, Gino," she began, but he ignored her and turned on Jaeger.

"Tell me, Shane," he snarled. "Just what made you change your celebrated contempt of the press? Is it that this journalist is in more attractive form and it suits your purpose?"

"Jaclyn, what is he talking about?" Shane asked her.

"Yes, Jaclyn, tell us," Gino urged, enjoying himself.

She sighed. "He's trying to tell you that I'm a journalist," she said quietly.

"You're *what*?"

Jaclyn jumped. "I'm here to interview Sophia," she said succinctly, flinching when he slammed his fist down on the railing beside her.

"Just when were you going to tell me that you are one of those gossipmongers?" he thundered. "When you had picked up some juicy little item of information about me from our conversation? Were you going to publish a little blurb, maybe entitle it 'I Had a Romantic Rendezvous with Shane Jaeger'?"

The contempt in his voice was as chilling as the now cool breeze from the ocean. Gino's untimely intrusion meant Jaeger would probably never believe that she was going to tell him, but she had to try.

"Look, I don't work for that kind of magazine," she began, trying to ignore the smirking Gino at her side. "I was going to tell you before—"

But she was talking to Jaeger's stiff, retreating back as he strode across the balcony and opened and shut the glass doors behind him with great force. Jaclyn turned back to stare at the ocean, but the scene swam before her tear-filled eyes.

"Jaclyn, *cara,* I'm sorry," Gino apologized, attempting to put his arm around her shoulders.

She shrugged him off. "Please, don't say a word. I can't believe what you just did. How *could* you?" She turned to face him, furious.

Gino swirled the remains of his drink in his glass and stared moodily into it. "I don't know," he said finally. "Seeing the two of you out here chatting away, when I'd been searching for you, did something to me."

"Must you be so jealous of him?" she demanded. "We weren't doing anything. Not that it's any of your business."

"I know, but just the thought of Shane Jaeger with you . . . He did it last year, and now he's trying to take someone away from me again—"

"Take me away from you?" she interrupted incredulously. "Gino, you and I only met again this afternoon. How can you think you have any claim on me?"

"Well, it's just that last year—"

"I don't care what happened last year. What do the two of you do, get together here each year to fight over women, or race? And we were talking about me!" she cried indignantly.

He shrugged and looked a little like a chastised child.

"Oh, what's the use!" She turned and left him. But her anger faded as she felt the keen interest of people standing near the sliding doors when she reentered the room just moments after Jaeger. Her cheeks hot with embarrassment, Jaclyn made her way to the ladies' room.

"Jaclyn, where have you been?" Sophia cried, turning around on a seat before a mirror. "Did Gino find you?"

50

Jaclyn sank down on the chair next to Sophia. "He certainly did. I was talking with Shane Jaeger at the time." She pulled a comb out of her evening purse and began to attack her breeze-tossed hair.

Sophia frowned. "That doesn't sound so good."

Jaclyn found herself confiding in her friend.

"Gino does tend to be possessive," Sophia agreed with a sigh. Her dark eyes probed Jaclyn's face. "I take it you don't care for my brother, then?"

"I do, but as a friend," Jaclyn emphasized.

Sophia shook her head sadly. "I don't think Gino wants you for a friend. And it would have been so nice if . . ." She trailed off a little wistfully.

"If what?"

Sophia grinned, a mischievous glint in her eyes. "Well, you'd do nicely as a sister-in-law."

Jaclyn laughed. "You're as impossible as your brother, do you know that?"

"I almost forgot to tell you," Sophia said as they walked back to the party. "I was talking to someone about your doing an article about me, and she asked to meet you. Oh, there she is."

"Me?" Jaclyn was surprised. "Why?"

"Jaclyn! Do you think no one reads your work and remembers your name?" Sophia chided her.

"Miss Taylor, I'm so pleased to meet you!" a plump, expensively dressed matron told Jaclyn when Sophia introduced them. "I've been reading your book, and I want to tell you that I love it!"

"Book?" Sophia looked confused. "I thought you wrote magazine interviews, Jaclyn?"

"The book is just a small collection of them." Jaclyn shrugged.

Her admirer waved away Jaclyn's modesty with a hand laden with diamond rings. "I'd hardly call it that. The book is called *Not Always Famous,* Miss Spinnelli. You shouldn't miss it. It's especially good." Her favorite interview, the woman told them, was the one written about a certain veteran actor.

Jaclyn laughed ruefully and had to confess that she never felt it was as good as it could have been. She'd been too nervous because of the actor's tremendous reputation. So much had been written about him that she was afraid she would blunder and not get a good interview. And she had feared that she couldn't write anything about him as good as she had read. Her editor had been pleased with it, but she still had misgivings about it to this day.

"Well, I loved it," the woman reiterated. "Of course, he's always been a favorite of mine. Tell me, are you going to try to interview that elusive Shane Jaeger while you're here?"

"Who?" She pretended not to notice the gleam in the woman's eyes.

"Shane Jaeger," she repeated. "I just saw him a few minutes ago." Her eyes moved toward the balcony doors to show Jaclyn that she had seen her return behind Jaeger to the room.

Jaclyn felt her face redden. "No, I'm not. I don't think most actors are worth the space in the magazines I contribute to. Especially him!"

"Oh?" The woman's eyes gleamed with anticipation as she moved closer. "Then you don't like Mr. Jaeger?"

Jaclyn was too angry to realize that she was being encouraged to vent her wrath, something she didn't normally do. "I found him to be insolent and totally uninteresting!" she said rashly, hearing Sophia gasp, but ignoring

52

her. "I mean, he's so Hollywood, so plastic, don't you think? Such a manufactured-sounding name, too—Shane Jaeger. And all this about his not liking the press. You'd think we acted like the paparazzi in Sophia's Italy, when most of us in this country are perfectly respectable journalists. I think the whole thing is his press agent's idea to get him *more* publicity, not less!"

"Is that so?" a voice spoke behind her, cold as ice and horribly familiar.

Jaclyn turned slowly to stare into the face of the man himself. His gray eyes glittered, his jaw was rigid with anger, and his knuckles showed white on the hand holding his drink, threatening to break the glass. The man exuded a dangerous air of barely controlled violence.

"Oh, Signor Jaeger, I have been dying to meet you!" Sophia rushed into the awkward silence, offering her hand and smiling at him with all her Spinnelli charm.

He was forced to acknowledge her, and then Jaclyn's fan, too, who was watching the whole scene with avid eyes. But when Sophia turned to introduce Jaclyn without thinking, his politeness vanished.

"I've already met the charming Miss Taylor," he said shortly.

"Oh, of course," Sophia gulped.

"I—I—" Jaclyn stammered. "You weren't meant to hear that. I mean—" She searched helplessly in her mind for something to say, some way to apologize. It was all too embarrassing. She stared down at her hands, twisting them together nervously. But when she looked up a moment later, she saw that he was enjoying her discomfiture. The man was actually smirking! She drew herself up and looked him in the eye, saying, "But then again, eavesdroppers never hear good of themselves, do they?"

She watched his smirk fade. "Point taken, Miss Taylor. But I wasn't eavesdropping. I had come over to introduce myself to Miss Spinnelli before I left the party. I was not anxious to hear your misinformed opinion of me. I was forced to listen to it. And," he continued relentlessly, "Hollywood name though it may sound, Shane Jaeger is my real name. Oh, and another thing. I neither disdain nor desire publicity, Miss Taylor. There's a line that exactly sums up my feelings. 'Frankly, my dear, I don't give a damn!' "

"Oh, Mr. Jaeger." The plump matron sighed worshipfully. "I just *know* you could play Rhett Butler in *Gone With the Wind* much better than Clark Gable did. Will you be in the sequel that I hear is going to be made?"

The actor dragged his eyes from Jaclyn's face, to stare disbelievingly at the woman for a moment. He shook his head slightly, as if to clear it, then quelled her interruption with a cold stare.

When he turned back to her, Jaclyn rushed to speak before he could begin again. "Listen, I'm not going to stand here and have a slinging match with you," she told him furiously. "I've already heard your slurs against my profession, *and* me, and I've had enough! Excuse me," she said to the others, pointedly excluding Jaeger.

She turned on her heels and stalked over to the buffet table, where she stood, staring unseeingly at the centerpiece, a carved ice sculpture of a race car.

"I really riled you, didn't I?"

She spun around and found that Jaeger had followed her.

"I'd appreciate it if you'd leave me alone," she said, her eyes glittering as icily as the frozen sculpture on the table.

He chuckled. "I seem to recall having said that a few

times myself," he replied evenly. "If you get so indignant at hearing what you think are slurs against yourself and your profession, then how do you think *I* feel about what's been said about me?"

"Well, I don't write that sort of trash!"

"Prove it!" he challenged.

"What?"

"Prove that you don't. I'll give you an exclusive interview, and you can show me you people aren't all alike."

She searched his face for some sign of sarcasm, but there was none. He was deadly serious.

"I—I—" she stammered.

"Chicken?" he taunted.

"No!" She drew herself up indignantly. "I have an assignment right now, anyway. About Sophia, remember? I haven't the time, and I'm certain I have no desire to interview you, anyway!"

"Why not?"

She looked heavenward. "Look, if nothing else, we'd never be able to talk to each other long enough without arguing to get anything to print."

"I thought you were a 'professional,' " he jibed sarcastically.

"I *am*!" she burst out so loudly that those people who weren't already watching their argument with curiosity took notice.

"Look." She lowered her voice. "After I finish with the piece about Sophia, I intend to take a vacation here. The thought of having a slinging match with you, or even being in the same city with you any longer than I have to, just doesn't appeal to me."

"Oh, that's right. You have no reason to go rushing off

55

after the race," he remembered. "Then you *can* stick around for a while." It was a statement, not a question.

"But I just said—" she began, exasperated.

He cut her off with a wave of his hand. "I'm going to make you prove yourself, Miss Taylor," he said softly. He moved closer, a threatening look on his face. "I think we'll both benefit from this little experiment."

"I'm not—"

"Yes, you are," he told her, his voice low and dangerous. The light from the chandelier was behind him, so that his face was partly shadowed. Jaclyn shivered slightly as she looked up into the glittering eyes staring down at her, gunmetal-gray and hard. "I can make you."

"You can't make me do anything!"

"I can put pressure on your magazine; tell them I offered you an exclusive interview. I'm sure they'd do anything for it. But I'll tell them the deal is off unless you cooperate," he said in a silky voice.

"I work as a free-lancer!" she shot back triumphantly.

"Then I'll just announce tomorrow that I've agreed to give you an exclusive interview, and we'll see what happens."

She gulped. She'd be inundated with offers.

"Well?" He waited.

"Checkmate, Mr. Jaeger." She lifted her head as she spoke the words of surrender.

He smiled. "Then I'll see you after the race. It shouldn't take more than a few days, should it?"

"No," she admitted. Then an idea came to her. She looked up at him, her eyes sparkling with malice. "But it could. I may have to dig very deep to find something interesting about you for the article. I remember someone

56

once put it so well. He said, 'Even a hero becomes a bore after a while.' "

"Why you little—" he began, but she escaped him then.

She'd probably pay for having provoked him. But it was worth it!

CHAPTER THREE

It was no good brooding about it, Jaclyn told herself angrily. But she kicked at a mound of sand before her and scowled anyway.

It was early, and the beach was deserted. She hadn't slept much after she had returned to her room late from the party the night before. She'd tossed and turned, thinking of the confrontation with Shane Jaeger, and finally had despaired of getting more sleep. Pulling on jeans and a thin sweater, she had taken a towel and walked down to the beach to watch the sunrise.

The sun rose, its rays turning the morning-gray sea into liquid aquamarine. Tiny brown-and-white sandpipers ran like windup toys, playing catch-me with the lapping waves. A lone pelican hovered, and then swooped into the deep-blue offshore depths, emerging with a breakfast fish in his beak.

Farther down the beach an old man appeared, bent over, sweeping the newly washed surface of the sand with a metal detector. He found no pirate treasures, only ordinary objects left behind by careless sun worshipers—a key ring and a cigarette lighter.

A young girl came to sit cross-legged and sketch the

quiet morning scene, scorning the camera that lay beside her on her towel.

Jaclyn lay back and closed her eyes as a sea breeze, fresh and salty, blew over her. The sound of the waves was soothing, and even the screeching of gulls overhead couldn't break the peaceful spell.

The steady sound of moving feet neared her, someone out for an early-morning jog. The footfalls stopped, and a shadow fell over her. She opened her eyes, which widened in surprise. She sat up abruptly.

"You!" she burst out.

It was Shane Jaeger. "Out early—or late, Miss Taylor?"

"Ooh," she groaned. "And it was such a perfect morning."

"Exactly what *I* thought," he retorted. He stood, his feet planted apart in the sand, his hands on his hips in an aggressively masculine posture. He was dressed in a navy-blue jogging outfit, the jacket unzipped nearly to the waist, revealing a bronzed, muscular chest.

His eyes were as cold and gray as the morning sea had been before the sun had dissipated the mist, and no less hard and scornful than the night before. They roamed over her body, lingering on her pale-yellow sweater and faded blue jeans.

She was conscious that she looked tousled, with her hair blowing golden and free in the breezes, and sand on her clothes. "Go away and don't spoil my morning," she said testily.

He raised a dark eyebrow. "Touchy this morning, aren't you?"

"We can't all be so disgustingly chipper in the morning, you know," she snapped.

"Especially when you apparently didn't sleep so well, eh?"

She glared at him. "Go—jog into the ocean or something, will you? Thanks to you, I'll have less time for the beach than I planned. So let me enjoy it now, okay?"

"Do you want to cancel our little deal?" he asked quietly.

"Yes!"

"Forget it!" he returned unequivocally, dashing her hopes.

"I told you last night," Jaclyn said between clenched teeth, "that I'll find some way to make you regret it if you force me to stay and interview you."

"What? And reinforce my opinion of the profession to which you're so loyal? That would make me right about you people, wouldn't it?" he sneered.

"I don't give a—I mean, I don't care about your opinions. And I don't like being forced into anything!" she retorted hotly.

"No?" he questioned. He lowered himself to the sand to sit too close to her. "When you can sell the piece to the highest bidder and make yourself a tidy profit?"

Outraged, she raised a hand to slap the derisive smirk off his face. But he was quicker than she, blocking off the assault and grasping her wrist with cruel, biting fingers.

"Oh, you're hurting me!" she cried, tears of anger and pain filling her eyes. She glared at him, a look of green-eyed contempt, but he seemed impervious to her glittering disdain.

"Did you really think I'd let anyone, even a woman, hit me?"

"Let me go, you macho egotist!" she demanded hotly. She tried to jerk away from him but only succeeded in hurting her wrist more. Her struggles sprayed them both with a fine shower of sand. Then suddenly she was on her back. She lay there, stunned for a moment, and his head and shoulders blocked out the sun as he stared down at her.

"Let me up!" she cried.

His mouth swooped down on hers, and he pressed a hard, punishing kiss on her lips. For a startled second she couldn't believe what he was doing. Then she renewed her struggles.

His kisses became gentler, persuasive. A shiver ran up and down her spine as the caressing warmth of his mouth awakened a response within her, and suddenly she didn't want to struggle anymore. Just as suddenly he released her lips, raising his head to stare down into her eyes.

"How dare you!" she managed to whisper.

He removed the crushing weight of his body from hers and sat watching her as she scrambled to her feet.

"You seemed to enjoy yourself," he said in arrogant unconcern.

"Enjoy myself?" She looked at him, incredulous. "Why, you—you mauled me!"

"You're just annoyed that you enjoyed my kisses and you stopped resisting." He grinned, unrepentant and got to his feet and brushed the sand from his sweat suit.

"See you later," he called over his shoulder as he jogged away.

Jaclyn watched in something of a daze as his figure moved down the beach. She shook her head, unable to believe what had just happened. There was movement to her side. The girl! She had seen everything! Jaclyn closed her eyes in embarrassment, and opened them to see the girl stuffing her things into a beach bag before hurrying off.

Jaclyn blushed as she remembered what the girl had witnessed. Just another reason to make me hate that maddening Shane Jaeger, she thought angrily as she walked back to her room to shower and change for breakfast.

Later on she was too busy following Sophia around in a mad rush of conferences with the crew chief and mechanics, and other details, to notice either Jaeger or Gino. Taking copious notes, she trailed behind the seemingly tireless woman racer, her tape recorder helping when she couldn't scribble Sophia's answers quickly enough.

When Gino met up with them for a hurried lunch, she ignored the entreaty in his eyes. Let him suffer a little for his behavior last night, she thought uncharitably.

He drove them back to the hotel and tried to detain Jaclyn, but she pleaded tiredness and escaped to her room. She was exhausted, and glad to see the day nearly over. Now, perhaps, she and Sophia could relax over dinner and talk a little more. But only a few minutes later Sophia was on the telephone, telling her about another party that night.

"Not another one, Sophia!" Jaclyn protested. "I'm bushed. Don't you ever slow down?"

"No one ever misses one of Mitch Corbin's parties. He's a real character, Jaclyn. You'll love him, and it may be the only time we'll get to talk during the next couple of days."

"Oh, all right. When?"

"Gino will tell you at dinner. I have night practice, so I'll join you later, okay?"

"But—" Jaclyn began, only to realize that Sophia had already hung up.

She tried to be cool toward Gino at dinner and during the ride to the party, but it was apparent that he meant to win her over. As soon as they got to the party he managed to get her outside, in a secluded corner of the patio. He put a lot of effort into apologizing as sincerely as he could. Gino used his soft, seductive charm to win her over in a manner carefully honed after many years of disarming others—children, parents, and teachers. The winsome little boy had turned into a charmer who, when he thought he had wrapped Jaclyn around his finger, managed to entwine strong adult arms around her waist. He murmured endearments in her ear, brushing away with his warm mouth the silken wave of hair that covered it.

"Say you'll forgive me, *bellissima,*" Gino whispered. The nearness of his mouth to Jaclyn's nearly swayed her from her anger. But she couldn't stand jealousy.

"Wait a minute." She disengaged herself from his embrace. His charm was potent, but she wouldn't allow herself to give in so easily. "You're going too fast, Gino."

"*Cara,* I—"

"No. I'll accept your apology because you said you had a little too much to drink last night. But I don't want to get this involved with you, Gino. I'm fond of you," she went on, looking at him levelly, "but I don't want you to get the idea that I'd like an affair with you while we're here."

"Jaclyn!" He stared at her with reproach in his velvety brown eyes. "I wouldn't offer you an affair, *cara.* You're not that kind of girl." He ran a finger down the curving line of her cheek. "Not that you look innocent in that Greek-goddesslike dress."

Jaclyn glanced down at her dress. The stark white crepe wrapped around her breasts and fell in graceful folds to her feet, an illusion of a cunningly draped towel with its figure-molding flattery and stylish simplicity. The whiteness set off her pale-peach skin. Her hair seemed a darker and richer gold as it brushed her shoulders in a simple style.

Gino moved closer, caressing her bare shoulders with warm hands. But she couldn't warm to his touch. His caresses, his endearments in a whispered mixture of Italian and English, seemed just a little too practiced. Then, too, she didn't care for his mercurial moods—from bitter accusation and jealousy last night to this soft persuasion and lovemaking tonight. Something was wrong, and it puzzled her.

When he kissed her again she knew what it was. The memory of a kiss from another man early that morning flashed through her mind. The memory of her response scared her, even while another man's lips were on hers.

Both men were masterful in their kisses. But Shane's lips had possessed a sensual power to draw a response from her and bring her pulsatingly alive. Gino would be furious if he knew what she was thinking while he kissed her.

Gino released her and stood back. He frowned. "You're a Greek goddess all right. Cold as a marble statue. What's the matter?"

She sighed and shook her head. "I'm sorry, Gino. I tried to tell you I only wanted to be friends with you. Anything else is impossible."

"Why?"

She sighed. "I thought you understood, you and Sophia, more than anybody. I just won't get involved with anyone with the kind of career you have."

"But you came here. I thought that meant you'd changed." Gino was confused.

"I'd have to share you with your mistress, don't you see? I couldn't do that," she said quietly.

"Mistress? Who could want another woman, *cara*?" he asked, drawing her into his arms again.

"You could be faithful to me?"

"Of course," he promised.

"Forever?"

"Jaclyn!" He was becoming exasperated. "Look, why extract a promise of fidelity? I'd try very hard, but no man can guarantee anything, can he?"

She smiled bitterly. "I don't think *you* can really promise that, even in the beginning, not to see another woman —or your mistress."

"What on earth are you talking about?"

She looked at him with troubled eyes. "I can compete with another woman, Gino. But not with your metal mistress."

"Oh, Jaclyn, don't start on that, not tonight." He rubbed his cheek against hers, and she inhaled the heady scent of his male cologne. "Your vulnerability attracts me, and yet I know I should do all I can to—"

"I hate to interrupt this tender scene." The man's tone of voice belied his apologetic words.

Startled, they both turned to face the intruder. An angry Shane Jaeger stood before them.

"What do you want, Jaeger?" Gino began belligerently.

"I suppose this was your idea of revenge?" the man spat at Jaclyn, ignoring Gino. He threw something at her feet in a gesture of disgust.

It was a newspaper. She bent and picked it up. Puzzled, she opened it. A startled exclamation escaped her lips as she saw the picture splashed across the front page.

It was slightly out of focus, as if taken in a hurry and

by an amateur, but entirely recognizable as a picture of Shane and herself kissing passionately.

"How did this get in here?" she gasped in horror.

Gino snatched the paper from her nerveless fingers as she stared incredulously at Jaeger.

"Oh, come on, you know very well," he sneered at her. "What I can't figure out is how you could have planned it. I had no idea anyone knew I jogged on the beach each morning at that hour."

"What is this, Jaclyn?" Gino's voice was ugly with accusation.

She dragged her eyes away from Jaeger's livid face to stare in disbelief at Gino. "I didn't have anything to do with this!" she protested. "Surely *you* believe that!"

"Are you saying this isn't you in the picture?" Gino demanded.

"Yes—I mean no—I mean I didn't have anything to do with that picture being taken!" she answered, confused.

Neither man appeared to believe her. And instead of being angry at his rival for kissing Jaclyn, Gino appeared to be blaming her! He threw the newspaper down and stood, hands on his hips in an accusing posture, glaring at her. Jaeger looked as if he longed to get his hands on her throat.

"I swear I don't know how this happened!" she continued in an effort to convince the two of them of her innocence. "I can't imagine who took it. We were the only ones on the beach." She frowned and chewed on her lower lip as she tried to think. "Wait a minute! There was a girl who was sketching, and she had a camera beside her. It must have been her!"

"Oh, sure!" Jaeger's tone was derisive.

Jaclyn stamped her foot in anger.

Jaeger stood in the shadows of the patio, and in the darkness his face looked satanic, yet he wore a grin.

"What's so funny?" she demanded.

"Be careful. I don't know how that strapless dress is staying up, but I'd enjoy seeing—"

"Oh, shut up! I've about had enough of the both of you acting like two little boys," she flared. "You two act like I enjoy being splashed all over the paper like that. I've never been so embarrassed in my life. *I've* never been pictured like that. Can the two of you say that?" She threw the accusation at them, and they exchanged a look she couldn't interpret. "Oh, you're impossible!" she burst out, annoyed at the lack of response.

"Who? Me?" Jaeger asked in a silken tone. "After seeing that picture, even Gino wouldn't think you felt that way, would you, Spinnelli?" He laughed and strode off. Jaclyn realized that he had had his revenge as Gino stepped closer angrily.

Jaeger had known instinctively that she'd have a hard time explaining to Gino what had happened that morning. Gino would never believe the truth. All he knew was that condemning black-and-white photograph. How could she explain how she and his rival had come to be kissing like—like illicit lovers?

It wasn't difficult, it was *impossible* to get Gino to see her side. How clever Jaeger had been! Jaclyn fumed. He was giving her more and more reason to dislike him. And she really didn't need more! First there had been the scene at the party the night before, on the balcony and then inside. Then the beach in the morning. And now. The threat of the interview, too, continued to hover over her head like the black cloud that followed those newspaper comic-strip characters wherever they went.

When a still-angry Gino stomped back to the party, Jaclyn watched him go with a mixture of disgust and relief. She went inside a few minutes later, hoping that she wouldn't be noticed. The night before, the partygoers had been treated to a procession of angry people entering the room, and had had plenty to speculate about the trio.

"Haven't we met somewhere before?" a man asked her. "I didn't mean that the way it sounded," he apologized.

She smiled. "Okay, what *did* you mean?"

He frowned and pushed back his black Stetson with his forefinger. He wore an expensively cut suit, but the combination of the hat, seldom seen at a fancy party, and his hands seemed incongruous. They were calloused, as if he did manual labor of some sort.

"I'm Mitch Corbin."

"Jaclyn Taylor," she introduced herself. "Didn't I see you in Shane Jaeger's pit area earlier today?"

"Sure thing. I always like to be around when Shane races—offer a little help if it's needed. Say, why haven't you got a drink? We'll have to get on to those fancy waiters walkin' around here and get you one."

"No, thanks," she said quickly.

"Sorry, shoulda thought you might not want one."

"It's just that I didn't feel right having one before I met the host."

"Well, you just met him." Corbin grinned.

"Oh, I'm sorry." She bit her lip, embarrassed. She'd have remembered this was *him* if she hadn't been angry.

The grooves on each side of his mouth deepened. "Shucks, honey, no problem. Now, why don't we go get you that drink? I'm feelin' a bit parched myself."

He was so pleasantly homey and down to earth, she felt as if she had known him for longer than a few minutes.

68

After shooing the bartender aside he moved behind the bar and asked what was the lady's pleasure.

"You were in stockers, weren't you, Mr. Corbin?"

"Call me Mitch. Sure thing. Seems like a long time ago."

Jaclyn leaned her elbows on the bar and watched him fix her daiquiri. "Yeah"—she slid into a Southern drawl—"I reckon you must be gettin' on now."

His head shot up at her words, his eyes narrowing, until he saw the gleam in her eyes and the laughter she was trying to hold back.

"How 'bout that, sneakin' up on ole Mitch like that." He chuckled. "I reckon it just seems like a long time ago with all these young folks around the tracks today. Heard someone funnin' one of the older drivers here today, callin' him a member of the 'over the hill gang.' Here"—he held out her drink—"see if that's to your likin'!"

She took it and sipped it appreciatively. "Lovely, thanks."

Mitch walked around the bar and joined her. "Now, if we could just find a place to set a spell. My wife keeps sayin' we don't need a big place like this, but it sure seems mighty small, times like this. Let's go in here," he said, opening a door that led into a very masculine-looking den.

Wall after wall was covered with photographs of cars, from cumbersome-looking models from the dawn of the automotive age to the stockers a young Mitch was pictured beside. And there were more than a few pictures of Shane Jaeger.

"Why did you give it up?" she asked.

"Ole ticker was givin' me trouble," he told her. "Yup, that's me," he said as she looked closely at a picture of a

69

car turned upside down, the driver still trapped inside. "Felt like a durned turtle, sittin' like that, 'til I got out."

"What's this?" She stared at a brick on a table.

"That's what I do now. See, there's a plaque on the wood base. Says it's a brick from the old Ormond Garage. The first cars that raced here on our beach were set up there. The drivers used to come back from the beach and paint their speeds on the inside walls. It was one heck of a place. They were fixin' to make it what folks call a historical landmark when it burned down. Now we're sellin' bricks from it to finance the museum of speed I help out at. Like to buy one?"

"It would make a nice gift, I suppose. Maybe for my cousin. He's interested in racing. How much are they selling for, Mitch?"

"Oh, a thousand a brick," he told her casually.

She choked on her drink. "Yes, I'll bet you *would* like to sell me one," she said, laughing. "I think that's a little beyond my gift budget. Tell me, have you sold many?"

"Oh, a respectable lot. Mostly to local businessmen and such who want to support what we're doin'. You know," he said, "I can't get over you lookin' like someone I knew. But then, you'd have been just a little thing back then. Can't figure it out. Wish my wife, Maggie, was here. She'd know. Got a mind for names and faces. She's saved me from makin' more of a fool of myself than I am many a time. Couldn't be here for our annual party. Our daughter's about to have a baby. Ole Mitch is gonna be a granddaddy for the first time."

"How nice," Jaclyn said, smiling.

"Have I met you at a race?" he questioned suddenly. She shook her head. "No. I haven't been to one for

70

years." But the more she looked at him, the more she recalled a fleeting memory of him.

"It would have been longer ago than that. Hey, here comes Shane!"

"Hello, Mitch. How's it going?" The deep voice spoke at her back. "Good evening again, Miss Taylor."

Groaning inwardly, she turned around. "Good evening, Mr. Jaeger," she said with a stiff smile on her lips.

"You two know each other?" Mitch wanted to know.

"You could say we have a passing acquaintance," he said dryly. "Don't you ever read the papers, Mitch?"

"Was she on the sports page? You know that's the only part of the paper I read, son."

"No." Jaeger appeared to smirk.

Jaclyn colored. "Excuse me, Mitch. I'd better go and find Sophia." But a hand restrained her.

"Why leave so soon?" There was mischief in Jaeger's eyes, a wicked tilt to his grin.

Jaclyn stiffened but decided to ignore him. As she walked away she could hear a low chuckle.

"There you are!" Sophia came toward her. "We go to the same party and I hardly see you. Just like last night."

"I'm sorry, I—"

"I know!" Sophia pulled her into a corner. "Now," she whispered conspiratorially, "what happened? Tell me what I missed?"

Jaclyn frowned. "What?"

"What did Signor Jaeger want? He was *so* angry!"

"Sophia! Did you send him out to the patio earlier?"

Sophia grinned, unabashed. "Of course!"

"How did you know where I was?"

Sophia shrugged. "I know my brother. I figured he had you in some secluded place and was flirting with you. You

71

know, I think I should be writing about you, not the other way around. You seem to be leading a far more interesting life than me lately. Jaclyn, did something happen before I got here?"

Jaclyn flicked her hair back casually. "Why do you ask?"

"People are staring at you again, like last night. Did I miss something?"

Jaclyn looked around her. Sophia was right. She hadn't noticed it before.

"Well?" Sophia's face was alight with curiosity.

Apparently she hasn't had a chance to see the newspaper tonight, Jaclyn thought. She caught a glimpse of Shane Jaeger and Mitch talking at the bar as she told Sophia the latest. What, she wondered, was Jaeger telling *his* friend?

That night, she lay awake for a long time, wondering what Jaeger would do to avenge that incriminating picture. By the looks she kept getting from him all night, she knew his anger hadn't cooled. Exhausted, she finally slept.

The next day Sophia had a free hour and she and Jaclyn walked on the beach. Jaclyn carried along her recorder and notepad, conducting a brief interview. Why, she asked, did Sophia want to compete in a sport so dominated by males? In such a dangerous sport?

"Why not?" she replied, shrugging her shoulders in a graceful movement. She shaded her eyes against the sun with a carefully manicured hand as she gazed out at the sea. "It is all I have ever known. Nothing else has ever captured my interest."

"And the danger?" Jaclyn persisted.

"Are you asking for the sake of the interview, Jaclyn?"

"Of course," Jaclyn told her. But her eyes fell before the woman's direct, steady gaze.

They climbed the steps from the beach to a large, open-air bandshell made of buff-colored coquina rock, and sat on one of the wooden benches that served as seats for seaside concerts.

"Is this not hard for you, asking these questions?" Sophia cross-questioned gently.

"I have to ask all sorts of questions. Embarrassing questions, rude ones—"

"No," Sophia interrupted. "You know what I mean. Is this not a painful line of questioning for you?"

"If it's important," Jaclyn said carefully, "I can ask anything of anyone. It's my job to stay as impartial and impersonal as I can." She stared out at the foam-capped waves as they flowed gently into shore, until the brilliance of the light reflecting off the water dazzled her eyes. "I think these are questions someone would want to ask," she told Sophia. "I write my interviews for the general public. I try to ask the questions people would ask the person themselves." She turned to face Sophia, her eyes glinting sea-green like the ocean, a mischievous smile playing about her lips. "I haven't even gotten to your love life yet. *Then* we'll see who gets pained at the questions!"

Sophia laughed, and a lighter mood prevailed as they walked back along the beach toward their hotel. She hadn't answered the question about the danger. But Jaclyn left it alone, unsure if Sophia was suspicious about talking of the dangers of racing, as many drivers were.

A toddler waddled on pudgy legs to the water's edge to crow delightedly at the waves, only to move quickly back as the water tried to wet her toes. She reminded Jaclyn of a tiny human version of the sandpipers she'd watched the morning before.

"I will get married one day, I hope," Sophia mused.

"I'm rather serious about someone right now. He wasn't able to come here at this time to watch me race."

"Then your racing isn't the all-consuming interest it is for some drivers?"

Sophia eyed her oddly but shook her head negatively. "It is possible to be consumed by my interest, especially a sport such as racing," she said slowly. "But it is also possible to have both the interest and a family. I value people, friendships, family, no less than anyone. Because I choose to participate in a sport such as this, that doesn't make me different from other women. I would imagine you stay as involved and busy with your work as I do with mine."

Jaclyn had to admit this was probably true. Especially lately, when she had been trying to work on a novel in between her free-lance work. It seemed sometimes that the more she wrote, the more she loved it. She couldn't understand the sort of love-hate thing some people made of writing. A blank page in her typewriter was a challenge, a free space in which she could wheel and soar and glide about like a sea gull.

For her, writing was a way to express herself. She was more introverted than most people and so had a more private area of interest. Her mother had claimed often to have had difficulty extricating Jaclyn from her typewriter, telling her daughter there were other things in the world. Jaclyn had often teased back that she couldn't imagine anything else more interesting. Not until she had met Shane Jaeger. He had— She had to stop herself from daydreaming.

Perhaps Sophia had a slight sensitivity to Jaclyn's questions. But surely Sophia had understood that Jaclyn meant many male drivers were so obsessed with racing that they ate, slept, *breathed* nothing but it? She pointed this out to Sophia, and her friend smiled.

"Perhaps I have a bit of a—what do you call it?" She searched for the appropriate American expression.

"Chip on the shoulder?" Jaclyn ventured hesitantly, and Sophia laughed.

"That's it," she agreed.

"Why aren't there more women race drivers?"

"We are a minority, true. But we have been racing almost since the first," Sophia replied. "There was one woman racer at the turn of the century. She used her maiden name in the race, for fear of embarrassing her wealthy merchant husband." Sophia told the story of another driver, a doctor, who had endangered her life and her standing in the race by stopping to aid an injured driver. When help arrived she jumped into the car her admirers had decorated with roses and lilacs and finished the race.

Women had had to race in the stiff corsets and bulky dresses of their time, she pointed out. Some women had played up their sexual difference by certain devices, calling attention to themselves. Sophia seemed to shudder when she told of cars painted pink, and so on. But today, she said, women downplayed their femininity and preferred to be considered as just other drivers.

Jaclyn had known that people were surprised to see how glamorous and womanly Sophia was. She'd noticed their reactions at the parties the last two nights and at the speedway. A woman who was in a male-dominated sport or activity was sometimes thought to want to look or act less feminine. But it wasn't often true, Jaclyn thought. Especially not in Sophia's case.

They were nearly at the hotel, and Sophia had to go. But she appeared to want to tell Jaclyn something else.

"Just one thing I want to add," she said finally, searching for words. "And not necessarily for the article, although I know I evaded that question you asked a while ago about the danger."

"Yes?"

"I'm going to be having a terrific time out there this weekend. A time I'll always remember. It's worth whatever risk there might be. Remember that, Jaclyn. It doesn't always end the way that your—I mean—oh, I'm putting it badly, I know. But remember, my uncle raced for years, only to be killed as he drove his family to a picnic along a quiet country road."

And then she was gone, leaving Jaclyn to stare after her.

CHAPTER FOUR

Race day! Jaclyn watched from her vantage point in the pit area as fans began filling the grandstands and infield. Today there was all the confusion of a big race, all the tension and excitement and the fevered hard work that had begun long before the opening ceremonies.

Gino and Sophia were too busy to do more than note her presence, although Jaclyn thought she detected a coolness in Gino's manner when he looked over at her. He wore an air of injured pride whenever he caught her eye. But he didn't approach her. She frowned, wishing she could forget the way things had been going between her and Gino—and Shane Jaeger.

Other people couldn't. She was aware of curious stares in her direction. The local paper apparently has a large readership, she thought wryly. She blushed again at the thought of that picture of her and Jaeger, splashed across the front page.

News of it had leaked out elsewhere, too. Neil Farrell had already called, offering to top anyone's offer for exclusive rights to an interview with Jaeger. He hadn't wanted to believe her when she tried to explain that she didn't want to interview the man. Oh, well, at least he hadn't cracked any bad jokes about her doing something else instead with the actor, she thought. He had too much class to say something like that. Or the shrewd business sense not to antagonize her, hoping she'd change her mind, or perhaps a combination of both.

She became aware of a flash of blue beside the Spinnelli area, and even before she looked over she knew that the man she was thinking about was standing there. Her eyes met his, and she shivered under the onslaught of his icy, forbidding expression. She wasn't sure if he looked more threatening in the bright sunlight or in the semi-shadows of the night when he had stood before her at Mitch's party and thrown the newspaper with that—that picture at her feet.

He turned and spoke with a young, obviously hero-worshiping crew member. She got the uneasy feeling that he was talking about her, confirmed when the youth looked in her direction and nodded. Hot color suffused her face, and she looked away quickly. Damn the man! she swore to herself.

"Excuse me, Miss Taylor?"

She turned to face the young crew member. "Yes?"

"Mr. Jaeger would like to speak with you after the race, ma'am," he said politely, beaming as though he were the bearer of a privileged invitation.

"Tell Mr. Jaeger to go to—" she blurted out, then caught herself, appalled. Why did this man seem to bring out her temper so?

"I mean, tell him I'm so sorry, I can't make it." She forced a saccharine smile to her lips as she spoke, and Jaeger watched her with a puzzled frown.

But she found it hard to maintain the artificial smile when her message was repeated and his face darkened. Maybe I shouldn't have done that, she thought uneasily, and her smile faltered. Then he was striding toward her, and she didn't have time for misgivings or fear. Within seconds he stood before her, his eyes glittering with rage.

Sensing something a little out of the ordinary, some emotional pyrotechnics instead of the mechanical variety they were accustomed to, the reporters surged around them as Jaeger took her arm and pulled her behind a stack of tires at the rear of the pit space. There was open curiosity on the reporters' faces about what would happen, she saw, and immediately she had a sinking feeling in the pit of her stomach. Even if this wasn't something to do with the race, they, and she, knew it would be news. Now she realized that she had made a mistake.

"I'm sorry, I was just kidding," she whispered quickly. "I'll talk to you later, anywhere. Please?" Anything to get these people out of here! she thought, her eyes sliding nervously around at the pencils poised above notepads, the cameras whirring, the smirks on those faces!

But he caught her intent. His eyes gleamed with amusement.

"Miss Taylor has something to tell you people," he drawled.

"W-what?" she stuttered as the crowd moved closer.

"Tell them about our little deal," he prompted ruthlessly. There was no humor in his voice or his eyes now.

"I—I—" she faltered.

"I've offered Miss Taylor an exclusive interview. Let's hope she has more facility with the written word than she seems to have with the spoken one." He chuckled.

There were groans and protests.

"Why didn't you give it to me, Shane?" one reporter asked. "I thought we understood each other."

"Don't worry, Hathaway. You'll get some other news

79

that will be just as exclusive," Jaeger promised. His tone was cryptic.

The reporter looked from the actor to Jaclyn and back again. Jaeger nodded imperceptibly, and the man seemed to understand—what? Jaclyn wondered nervously.

"What about us? Why her and not one of us?" someone was asking. There was a low murmur that Jaclyn couldn't understand. But snickers followed, and she could guess what had been said.

"I said you'd get more than you bargained for, didn't I?" were Jaeger's parting words. Before she could speak he'd turned and now was striding away.

The crowd of reporters moved in like a pack of hungry vultures.

"Well, what gives, Miss Taylor?"

"Why is he giving you the interview?"

"Just what is your relationship to Jaeger, Miss Taylor?"

"Where do you plan to *do* this interview?"

"Please, I—" she began, panic welling up in her as they crowded in on her.

"What's going on here?" Gino materialized at her side. "Are these people bothering you, Jaclyn?"

"Oh, Gino, please, tell them to go away," she begged in a low voice. "I can't cope with them, not at all!"

The reporters were dismissed with an imperious wave of his hand and a terse "Miss Taylor has nothing to say." Muttering "paparazzi" under his breath, he turned to her and placed a comforting arm around her shoulders. "Now, what was all that about?"

"Shane Jaeger set them on me," she said with a sigh.

His lips tightened. "Why?"

Jaclyn explained briefly. "Wait, where are you going?" she asked, alarmed.

"To straighten him out. I—"

"No!" She grabbed his hand. "Gino, no! I won't have a brawl!"

"But, Jaclyn—"

"No! I mean it! Besides, why did you rescue me? I thought you were angry, too?"

Gino shrugged his shoulders inside the scarlet driver's suit. "Well, I guess I was," he said sheepishly. "I didn't like to think that Shane might be your lover."

"Lover!" she burst out in disbelief. "Gino, nothing could be further from the truth, believe me!"

"No? Then how do you explain that picture?" His face twisted in a sneer.

"I told you last night! I—wait a minute, I'm not going to get into all that again. Not here. Not now. What am I saying? I don't have to explain anything to anyone, anytime."

"Oh, yes, you do, *cara*," he said, edging closer, his words soft and loverlike. But his eyes glittered, and suddenly, even with all the people around, she was frightened. "Never forget you are mine, Jaclyn. I won't let anyone take you from me again."

Stunned, she stared at him. "Gino," she said uneasily.

"Howdy, folks, how're you doin' today?" a gravelly voice inquired.

"Ah, Signor Corbin." Gino nodded stiffly.

"Mitch, call me Mitch, son. None of that seen-yore stuff." Mitch's smile was genial. "Say, son, I think they're a-tryin' to get your attention."

Gino looked over at his crew. "Yes, it seems so. Later, Jaclyn."

She shivered in spite of herself. What had been wrong with Gino?

Mitch was saying something. She dragged her attention away from Gino's retreating back. "I'm sorry, Mitch, what did you say?"

"Is there something wrong?"

"No, what could be wrong?" she said lightly. The wind blew a strand of hair across her face, and she tucked it nervously behind one ear. "It's a beautiful day for a race, isn't it?"

Mitch nodded, his blue eyes taking in the busy scene around them. "Can't seem to leave him alone, can they?" he drawled.

Jaclyn looked in the direction in which Mitch pointed with his unlit pipe. Everyone, or so it appeared, was taking pictures as the cars were prepared for the starting grid. A disproportionate number were grouped around the driver Mitch pointed out—Shane Jaeger.

"Don't rightly know how he can stand to have them flash bulbs a-poppin' in his face. Woulda drove me crazy before a race." Hands on hips, feet apart, he watched the activity in the Jaeger area with a touch of amazement on his weathered face.

"You must have had people doing that to you in your day."

"Not like this. That's what bein' a movie star will do for you, I guess. Listen, where you gonna be sittin' to watch the race? I'd like to talk with you some more."

"About what?"

"Oh, this and that," he said, noncommittally. Then, seeing she was curious, he told her he'd been thinking about getting her advice. "Been thinkin' 'bout writin' up a book for the museum. You know, a racin' history of the area."

"I'll be here in the pits most of the time," she told him.

"You won't be sittin' in the press box? Why not? That's where most of 'em hang out, especially when it gets a mite cool later on."

"I like to be closer to the action," she said with a shrug. That wasn't the only reason, she told herself. She'd do well to stay away from the press when she didn't have a body-guard like Gino. She remembered how he had acted just after he'd brushed the press off, and again felt a tremor of uneasiness. Why had she been afraid of Gino? He was a friend. . . .

"Sure you wouldn't like to sit up where the drivers' families sit?" Mitch was asking.

"No!"

He pushed his hat back to look more closely into her face, his eyes narrowing.

"No, thank you," she said more calmly. "Listen, Mitch, I'd really better be getting back to the Spinnellis. I'll see you later, okay?"

"Sure thing, honey, sure thing." He nodded.

She had the feeling that he watched her as she walked back to the Spinnelli space. There, a coin was being flipped, amid much laughter from onlookers, to determine which Spinnelli would start the race. Sophia won, made a mild protest that she shouldn't, then quickly got into the car before her brother could take her up on her halfheart-ed offer that he be the first.

Jaclyn stole a glance at the pit beside them. Mitch was helping Jaeger with his gloves, so apparently Jaeger was his team's starter. The actor looked up just then, caught Jaclyn's eye before she could look away, and winked broadly. Blushing, she jerked her head back and stared stonily ahead.

Soon the cars were being lined up. Before Sophia joined

them, Jaclyn gave her "their" signal of encouragement with a light manner and a smiling face.

Engines rumbled beneath gleaming hoods, painted colors both subtle and crayon bright. The lines of their bodies resembled runners anticipating a start, chests hunched close to the ground, tails high, aerodynamically designed to cut wind resistance and make the cars hug the road. The cars left pit road in a roaring pack, traveling one circuit. Then there was a blaze of green as the starter leaning over the track on a metal platform waved his flag—and the race was on!

Jaclyn felt the familiar surge of excitement as she watched the cars whip past—Ferraris, Porsches, Carerras, Mazdas, Corvettes, BMWs. There was an international mix of cars piloted by drivers just as international, with names like Angelo, Manfred, Yoshimi, Anatoly, Jean-Paul, Manuel, Brian and Bill. Their addresses were from all over the World—Paris, Brussels, Germany, Tokyo. And Shane Jaeger's alleged address of Hollywood, California.

Jaeger's car, as well as Sophia's, was one of those in the lead. But none of the drivers was pushing for excessive speed or jockeying unnecessarily for first position. All knew that in a twenty-four-hour endurance race such action was both unwise and unnecessary.

Hours later, most of the cars were still in the race. Some had taken time out only for quick pit stops. But as time passed, here and there a car failed for a minor or major reason and had to be hauled away ignominiously by an ordinary tow truck. Attrition was high in such a race, Jaclyn knew. As yet there had been no accidents, or even really close calls, unlike watching the hair-raising, bone-crunching stockers racing at two hundred miles per hour plus, that also were seen at the same racetrack.

When the engine of one car failed Jaclyn heard the tale passed down pit road of a factory team's manager paying an exorbitant sum for another from a team with one on hand. It wasn't hard to believe that he was willing to spend that incredible thirty thousand on the engine, when it was reported that one major manufacturer had put a half million into promoting that car at the race. Winning here meant capturing not only a prestigious international race but also worldwide publicity.

Caught up in the excitement of watching men and a sole woman guiding the magnificent machines around the twisting course, Jaclyn wondered how she had been able to stay away from it all for so long. The more she watched, the more she enjoyed it. She hadn't really thought it possible. Her ghosts were nearly dispelled. Only someone's casual comment that there hadn't been any crashes yet marred her enjoyment for a moment.

Laughter came from the Spinnelli crew, speaking with Sophia via the communications device built within her helmet. Jaclyn was able to make out that Sophia didn't want to return to exchange driving chores with Gino. She was having far too good a time to want to come in yet, she was saying. Gino sternly ordered her in so that she wouldn't overtire herself, then relented for "just a couple more laps, *bambino*."

Cars moved in and out of pit road with alarming speed. Often one pulled in and met another leaving, so drivers had to be even more alert there than on the track. As they merged with others on the course Jaclyn watched with especial awe. She'd often thought it took courage for the average street driver to do the same at much slower speeds on highways.

Daylight faded, and as darkness fell over the course, drivers switched on their headlights. Those and infrequently placed lights would be the only illumination for the drivers through the night. The car exhaust pipes glowed red with heat now, and white flashes spewed dragonlike from them as cars downshifted into turns, something the fans couldn't see in the daytime.

Eventually the Spinnellis changed places, as did Jaeger and other teams, taking advantage of food and drink and rest in campers parked behind the pits. A section was reserved for drivers, crews, and the large semi-trailer trucks that had transported the cars and assorted parts.

Jaclyn got up from her folding chair, stretched, and decided to take a stroll in the infield. Some race fans had cast her envious glances when she entered the pit section. But now she found that most were content to be "outside," where the race-going public dwelled. And for a very obvious reason. It was party time!

The brochure she'd sent for before flying down from New York had described the race and noted that some considered it "the world's largest party." And many people here evidently were trying to prove it!

Refreshments, mostly alcoholic, accompanied food being hungrily consumed. Everything from a snack or the prosaic sandwich to elaborate delicacies unpacked from woven baskets, was the order of the day. Diners sat on station-wagon tailgates, car hoods, and roofs. Some of the more elegant and better prepared had even brought along small tables and folding chairs.

The spectators proved as dissimilar as everything Jaclyn had observed about their vehicles and food. Ages ranged from a toddler wide-eyed with excitement, dressed in a jumpsuit with racing patches that proclaimed him "Kiddie Car Driver of America," to an elderly German gentleman who used a stout walking stick as he stepped about briskly.

Men eyed Jaclyn with a desire to get acquainted, but she was scarcely conscious of them. Her mind was on the man racing the cobalt blue car around the track, who had disturbed her so before the race. And not just *before* the race, either, she told herself.

Hers wasn't the only mind concentrating on Jaeger's car. Once she overheard a young girl saying plaintively, "Yes, but where is Shane's car?" when the male beside her tried to explain the race. Jaclyn wondered how many people were only interested in watching the actor race. She had noticed many cameras and binoculars trained in his car's direction each time it passed.

The duel between Jaeger and Gino sharpened as the night wore on. The two top places were being retained by an American team and a British one, while the two rivals exchanged third and fourth places repeatedly. Jaclyn found herself rooting for the Spinnellis. She was more than just hoping that her friends would do well, she had to admit to herself. Now she wanted them—or anyone—to best Jaeger. It would do him good, she thought moodily, to have some of that arrogant pride knocked out of him.

Her thoughts went back to the confrontation before the race, just the latest in a series of clashes that seemed to happen each time they met, and she felt a growing sense of frustration. There just had to be some way out of the interview, there had to be. If only she could find a way to back out, without losing face. . . .

Noise swelled around her as cars approached a nearby

turn and one car had trouble maneuvering it. Something could happen during the race to prevent their talking later, she mused. Then she realized what she was thinking. *My God!* That's the last thing I'd want! she thought, appalled. Why am I letting this whole thing get to me like this, make me think like this? she asked herself.

The leaders approached the turn, braking as they saw the car ahead of them in trouble. Two cars grew dangerously close—Gino's and Shane's, Jaclyn saw. They appeared to emerge unscathed, then the red Spinnelli car shot forward, and the second car veered into the concrete retaining wall. One side scraped against the wall before Shane was able to guide it away, into the center of the track, and down onto pit road.

The car bore a gash, edges streaked with bright red. Like blood, Jaclyn thought, and she shuddered as she stared at the scarlet paint on the cobalt metal "skin" of the car as Shane emerged to talk with Mitch.

Fragments of their heated discussion came across the din of the pit, punctuated by the bulletlike burst of noise made by a pneumatic air wrench used to change tires quickly. The implications of Shane's angry words hit Jaclyn with a force the air wrench wreaked on her eardrums.

"No charges . . . can't prove . . . Spinnelli . . ."

No, she couldn't be hearing right, she told herself, her eyes wide with horror. They couldn't be thinking that Gino had deliberately tried to make Jaeger crash, they couldn't! Backing away on shaky legs, she made her way to her chair at the rear of the Spinnelli space.

"Is something wrong, Signora Taylor?" a friendly mechanic inquired. He eyed her oddly when she shook her head, but he shrugged and turned back to watching the race.

Jaclyn got up and paced restlessly, unable to sit and think about the near accident, and the possibility that Gino might have been to blame. She shivered again.

"Loan you my jacket if you need it," a gravelly voice offered.

She looked up. "No, thanks, Mitch. I'm not really cold."

"That so? I thought I saw you shiver," he remarked. "I was just lookin' around for some coffee. Want some?"

"Yes, thanks. Where?"

"In the press box. They usually have fairly good stuff."

"I don't know." She hesitated. Since that skirmish earlier she was unsure if she should venture into the place where her peers congregated. She saw that Mitch was watching her. "I'm not sure I believe you about the quality," she said lightly. "The stuff at the magazine office is always pretty awful. You can't stir it with a stick, it's so thick and black."

He chuckled. "Now, *that's* coffee, like we used to have down at the garage. Been missin' it since I retired. Come on, see for yourself," he urged.

She grinned and gave in to his persuasion. "Okay," she said, starting to walk beside him.

Cars went past in a blur of color and sound. "Shane's doin' real well, ain't he? Oh, he ain't been watchin' the race through the rearview mirror, but you're not 'sposed to pour it on in this race like the stockers. He's been doin' damn good, that boy." There was a note of pride in his voice.

"I noticed you were a fan. From way back," she said dryly, gesturing toward his fraying jacket.

He grinned, finding no offense at her teasing words. "Now, woman, you sound like my wife, puttin' down my jacket like that. She's always threatenin' to put it in the trash bin. I'll admit I've been watchin' Shane since he first started racin'. Got a heap of talent, he does. Tried to get him to enter a few international races, I did, but he says he's too busy with them movies.

"Can't understand it myself," he said thoughtfully, striking a match to light his pipe. He could smoke now that they were clear of the pits and their ever-present fire dangers, where a firefighter stood, silent sentinel with his extinguisher, at each space. "I asked him once. I said, 'Shane, how can a man love two things?' "

"What do you mean?"

"Shane says he won't give up one thing for the other. If a race stands in the way of a movie he wants to make, then the race has to be forgotten. Now, I could never do that. Not for anything, not even when it caused problems in my family life more 'n once."

"Neither could most racers," Jaclyn agreed quietly.

"Have to agree there. Gets harder each year to stay away from it all. Those are pretty fancy pieces of racin' metal out there on the track right now."

"Metal mistresses," she murmured.

"What's that?" Mitch's voice was sharp.

"Er—nothing, Mitch."

"You said *metal mistresses*." He put a restraining hand on her arm, forcing her to come to a stop. "Now, where did you hear 'em called that?"

"I—don't know," she stammered, surprised at his sudden question. "I guess I must have picked it up somewhere. What does it matter?"

Mitch's forehead creased in thought; his faded blue eyes had a distant look. "Like hearin' a voice outta the past. Haven't heard 'em called that for—how long?" he asked himself out loud, puffing hard on his pipe so that his Stetson was circled by a wreath of smoke.

Jaclyn watched the ground beneath her feet as she walked, letting the wind-whipped strands of her hair hide her expression. Why hadn't she told Mitch the truth? she asked herself. How long was she going to hide away from her past, as if it were something disgraceful? Or, to be closer to the truth, as if it were something that could still hurt. She could cope with the curiosity, the—pity now, couldn't she? For a moment she was torn by indecision. Then it was too late to confide in Mitch, as he opened the door to the press box.

Inside, there was a clutter of tables and chairs. Here and there someone was hunched over a pad of paper or a tape recorder. Others stood about in groups, talking about the race.

"Hey, Jaclyn! I've been looking for you!" a voice called.

She watched the lanky form of Scott Green unfold from a chair.

"I see you have." Her tone was dry.

"Well"—he shrugged—"I had to take a break and find out what all that commotion was in the Spinnelli pit, like everyone else, didn't I? And I could never seem to find you to ask about it."

"Yeah, what was all that about?" Mitch wanted to know.

"I hear you and Jaeger had it out," Scott began, eager to tell her what he'd evidently learned.

"Uh, Scott, have you met Mr. Corbin?" she interrupted him hastily. "Mitch, this is Scott Green, a photographer sent here with me. Scott, this is Mitch Corbin, one of Mr. Jaeger's *friends*," she emphasized warningly.

Scott looked at her, took the hint, and straightened

respectfully. He put out a hand to Mitch, grinning. "Glad to meet you, sir, very glad. I should have recognized you."

Mitch made a deprecating shrug of his shoulders. "Didn't think any of you young folk remembered me," he said laconically.

"Are you kidding?" Scott asked, incredulous. "Who could forget the man called the king of the stockers? Why, you're a legend!"

Jaclyn thought she detected a gleam of satisfaction in Mitch's eyes.

"Sit here and I'll get you a cup of coffee," Scott told Mitch. He pulled out a chair for him, as if for royalty, completely ignoring Jaclyn, who found one for herself. "How do you take it, sir?"

"Call me Mitch, son. Black'll be fine."

Scott turned and rushed away.

"I'll have mine with a little sugar, please," Jaclyn called after Scott's retreating back. She wondered if he had heard.

Mitch grinned. "Nice young fella. Say, why do you suppose we're bein' stared at?"

Jaclyn looked around her. Mitch was right. They were being watched. Hot color flooded her cheeks.

"You—you were telling me the other night about your work with the museum," she said hurriedly. "I didn't get the chance to ask if you'd ever thought of writing it all down."

"You wouldn't be changin' the subject, would you?" His eyes twinkled. "But no, I'm no writer. Can't imagine no country boy like me a-tryin' to set down words all pretty on a page, not when I talk like I do, and all. I'd like to tell it all to someone, though, get them to write it all down. You wouldn't happen to be stickin' around after the race, would you? You understand racin'. You act like you know a little more than the average fan."

"Why do you say that?" Her green eyes were wary.

He shrugged. "Don't rightly know. Shane and I both think so. Like I said before, I'd swear I've met you before. You look and talk like someone I've met somehow. It's a puzzlement, that's what it is."

"I'm sorry, Mitch, I won't be here long."

Mitch chuckled. "That's not what Shane said." He reached for an ashtray and knocked out the contents of his pipe into it. "Didn't say why."

She sighed. "Well, we *have* had some discussion about an interview."

"Interview? You have an interview with Shane Jaeger?" Scott's voice, overloud with surprise, startled them. He set the cups of coffee down so quickly, some spilled on the table. "Does Mr. Farrell know?"

"Shh," Jaclyn hissed.

"Who's Mr. Farrell?" Mitch wanted to know.

"The owner of the magazine," Scott informed him. "Does he, Jaclyn?"

"No!" she said sharply. "I mean, it's not arranged yet, Scott. Mr. Jaeger and I might not be able to work things out." She took a sip of her coffee, hoping to forestall any more talk, and burned her mouth on the scalding liquid.

"Oh, don't pay her no mind," Mitch told Scott. "They may fool you, son, and they may be foolin' each other, but they sure ain't foolin' ole Mitch here. I reckon they'll be able to sort it all out. Most women fight for the chance to be near Shane."

Bright spots of color burned on Jaclyn's cheeks. "I'm not most women!" she retorted.

Mitch held up his hands. "Hey, now, don't get all het

up. Didn't mean no harm. But I'll still bet you'll be around a lot longer than you think," he said cryptically. Turning to Scott, he thanked him for the coffee, then rose. "Guess I'll be gettin' along now, see how Shane's doin'," he told them before ambling away.

"Shane, Shane, that's all I ever hear," Jaclyn muttered aloud to herself.

"What?" Scott asked.

"Nothing."

A gust of cool air signaled another entrant to the crowded room.

"Hey, Lindy, warm enough for you?" someone called out as a bundled-up figure shut the door behind herself.

"Very funny," came the sarcastic rejoinder as gloved hands pulled off a stocking cap, then a scarf—and a jacket and a sweater and another beneath it. Finally, off came her gloves, and she accepted a cup of coffee from one of the reporters, cradling it in her hands and breathing in the warmth from the steaming cup.

"Aren't you going to drink it?" someone asked.

She shook her head. "I can't stand coffee. I just came in to warm up. Can you imagine—I'm going to have to go back to the paper and make it sound near-bikini weather out here, or the Chamber of Commerce will be after me."

Scott and Jaclyn looked at each other. It wasn't *that* cold. Cool maybe, but not cold.

"Where are you from?" Scott asked curiously.

"Here. Why?"

"'Cause it sure isn't cold compared to where we come from," he told her. "It was in the twenties when we left New York."

The girl shivered. "Well, this is cold for us here. Say,"

she turned to Jaclyn, "aren't you the one Shane Jaeger is giving the interview to?"

"Uh, I'm sorry, I have to be getting back." Jaclyn stood up quickly. "See you later, Scott."

"What's with her?" Jaclyn heard Lindy asking Scott as she hurried outside.

It was light out now. People were moving about, getting coffee to wake them if they had been asleep, or just to keep them awake if they hadn't wanted to miss the action. And for some, the coffee was for the hangover they had from enjoying it all a little too much the night before.

Two mechanics were passing out doughnuts and coffee in the Spinnelli pits. "How's it going?" one of them, Luigi, asked cheerfully in a thick accent.

Jaclyn laughed. "I can see you've been picking up our expressions." She selected a doughnut from the box he held out, and accepted a cup of coffee from the other man. She hadn't been able to finish her cup in the press box in her haste to avoid the reporter.

The Italian grinned. "Sure thing." He rattled off a few more, to her delight, before he moved on, saying, "Let me know if you need anything. Gino told me to keep an eye out for you during the race."

Jaclyn wondered why as she bit into the doughnut. Had Gino thought the reporters might try to bother her again? Certainly Jaeger couldn't, not while he was occupied with the race. Except for that time when he had pulled into the pits after the near crash, Jaeger hadn't been aware of her at all each time he drove his car in, staring ahead unblinkingly as he awaited fuel or a tire change.

No, Gino's desire for Luigi to watch out for Jaclyn smacked more of overprotectiveness, or the jealousy that seemed to flare within him as quickly as his anger. But why? she asked herself. He wasn't in love with her, and he knew she wasn't with him. When he married, it would undoubtedly be to an Italian woman, one who understood his passion for racing. He knew Jaclyn didn't, and why.

She thought back to the time four years ago when she had last seen Gino. It had been the night of her eighteenth birthday, and the mood had been high and exciting. Jaclyn's father had given her the racer charm for her bracelet, and everyone had considered it a lucky sign that her birthday, his car number, and the day of his important race all numbered eighteen. His good luck symbol, he'd called Jaclyn, giving her a fatherly kiss and hug while the party looked on.

Gino had taken her for a drive after her birthday celebration. She had become a little frightened of Gino, who seemed to be driving too fast, had drunk too much, and wanted to take far too many liberties when she had talked him into pulling off the road. Jaclyn had hoped he would sober up, but instead she had ended up wishing she hadn't asked him to stop—or told her father about it later.

Jaclyn tried to remember details of that angry quarrel between the two men the next day, and couldn't.

The announcer's voice brought her back to the present, calling out the latest positions. The action had picked up. While the night hours were favored for adding a few extra laps because engines stayed cooler, now drivers knew there were only hours to go before the race would be finished. The cars that would drop out because of engine problems usually had done so by then. Only about half of the cars that had started were still running.

Lead changes were reflected on the lighted telesign. The all-American team still led, Shane and his co-driver, a Frenchman, had moved to second place, and a British

96

team was in third. Gino had fallen to fourth. A Japanese team was running well, and Jaclyn had seen their drivers often this past week. She had found the letters of their bloodtypes sewn on their uniforms—a chilling reminder of the danger of the sport.

Gino pulled in so that Sophia could have a turn driving. He looked in a bad temper and strode past Jaclyn with barely a nod in her direction.

"Signorina, please to tell Gino to come back. *Presto!*" a mechanic called to her urgently.

She rushed after him and stopped him on his way to the camper. He hurried back to the pits and huddled with the crew chief, who appeared to be more than a little upset about something. Uncertain whether to follow Gino back, or wait where she was on the chance that the two men would finish their conversation quickly and she could talk with Gino, she waited. Looking out on the course, she couldn't find Jaeger's car.

"Looking for someone special?" a voice inquired.

Startled, she spun around. "Certainly not you," she retorted, glaring at her tormentor.

Jaeger laughed, holding up a hand as if for protection. "It's a good thing I have a flameproof suit! I swear, those eyes of yours could burn a hole in me if I didn't! Hey, what's the matter, what did I say?" he asked when she backed away from him, her face turning pale.

"Nothing! Don't speak to me!"

"No need," he shot back. "I'll be seeing you. *Later.*" And then he strode toward his camper.

"What did Jaeger want?" Gino's voice was low, tense.

"Nothing. Is something wrong?"

"I want him to stay away from you!" Gino swiped at a mustache of sweat on his upper lip, his eyes narrowing

97

as he stared in the direction of Jaeger's camper. He flexed his shoulders in a nervous gesture and seemed distracted, and as if he had too much energy. Jaclyn spoke, but her words were unheeded.

"What did you say?" Gino asked, dragging his eyes back to Jaclyn.

"I said you should go get some rest, instead of worrying about him, okay?"

"I waited too long to have you again, *mi amore,*" he told her. "I won't have him interfering."

She bit her lip. Much as she wanted to tell him she wasn't, and had no intention of being, his, she didn't want to upset him during the race. Better to talk to him later and straighten him out, she decided.

A crew member walked past, carrying a box of parts. Gino watched him moodily, still not going to his camper. Then he brightened and flicked her under the chin with a cheery "See you later."

She walked back to the pits slowly, frowning at his abrupt change of mood. Scott was sitting in her chair when she returned. He got up, but her eyes were on the sandwich in his hand. "What's that?" she asked with interest, forgetting Gino.

"Got it over there," he gestured with one hand, his mouth full. "I'll go get you one if you want."

"No, I can get it myself. You can stay where you are until I get back." Busy unwrapping the sandwich as she walked, Jaclyn bumped into someone. "Sorry," she apologized, looking up. The man, dressed in a dirty mechanic's uniform, averted his face and hurried on. That's funny, she thought absently, biting into her sandwich as she returned to her chair. He seemed familiar somehow, even with the cap pulled down low over his face. Must be because he was one of Jaeger's crew, she thought, remembering the cobalt blue uniform the man had worn. She finished the sandwich and disposed of the paper. Wiping her hands on a napkin, she found herself staring at them.

That's what was odd, she thought suddenly. The mechanic's hands were clean, not dirty like his uniform. Oh, well, maybe he just washed them, she thought, dismissing the whole matter from her mind and reaching for her notepad.

Sometime later Jaclyn was making notes when she heard a noise that made her head jerk up, a familiar sound that meant something was amiss with an engine. A blue car came into view and appeared to be in trouble. It veered wildly across the track and ground its side against the wall. The impact sent it across the track, into the path of the oncoming cars.

There was a scramble to dodge the car, and each other, and then an explosion of sound and flame burst from the moving cluster of cars. A fiery blaze and acrid black smoke filled the air, obscuring the identity of the drivers and cars in trouble. Yellow caution lights flashed, and emergency crews went into action as the crowd went into an uproar.

Jaclyn strained to hear what the announcer, his voice excited, was saying about the cars involved. There were the names of Spinnelli and Fenton. And *Jaeger.* Terror leaped into her throat as she searched for some sign of a scarlet car. And a cobalt blue one. The blare of sirens from emergency vehicles and the noise of the crowd ricocheted around Jaclyn's head.

"No, no, not again! Please, God, not again!" someone screamed over and over, until Jaclyn felt her head would explode. She covered her ears with her hands, and shut her

eyes in an attempt to block out the awful noise of someone's hysteria.

She felt herself being roughly shaken, and opened her
eyes to find Luigi's hands on her shoulders. He pulled her
hands from her ears, and she heard the screaming again.
Then she realized that it was she who was hysterical, but
she couldn't stop until Luigi delivered a stinging blow to
her cheek.

She reeled under the shock and pain of it.

"I'm sorry, signorina," he apologized, guiding Jaclyn to
her chair. He looked stricken with concern. "I had to slap
you. I didn't know how else to stop you."

Dazed, she put a hand to her throbbing cheek, wiping
at her tears with the back of her other hand.

"It's all right. Gino wasn't involved," he reassured her
as she tried to look past him out onto the course.

"Who?" she asked urgently.

"It looks as if it's Jaeger. Hey, don't pass out on me!"

She tried to focus on his face, understand the Italian
words swirling around her head as the Spinnelli crew
hovered around her. *Medico.* That meant doctor. *Un
sedativo*—sedative.

"Come on," Luigi said gently, helping her up. "Let's go
over to the infield hospital."

"Why are we going there? You said Gino wasn't hurt!"

"He isn't. I think you'd better have a doctor look at
you." Despite her protests, he put an arm around her and
helped her through the throng of concerned faces.

The scene on the track was still bedlam. Firemen were
hosing down a jumbled mass of blackened metal, while
caution lights seemed to scream yellow in Jaclyn's brain.
Even without asking Luigi, Jaclyn knew that the lifeless-

100

looking body being pulled from the still-smoldering wreckage was Jaeger's.

It was so much like another time, in another place. Guilt pulled at the frayed edges of her nerves as she blamed herself anew. Didn't I think about how I could get out of the interview and another confrontation with Shane if something happened to him during the race? she accused herself. And what about the tension I seemed to provoke between Jaeger and Gino? It's no better than last time, she cried in her mind. Have I jinxed another man, killed him as surely as if I had held the murder weapon?

Memories clawed to the surface, sharp talons of remembered tragedy ripping her apart again mercilessly as the two scenes became confused in her mind, came together and shifted apart in a kaleidoscope of horrible pieces.

"No!" she sobbed, and felt herself propelled more firmly toward the infield hospital by the strong arms of a man who didn't understand what was happening to her.

CHAPTER FIVE

Jaclyn sat on the hard examining table, alone in the curtained-off room in the infield hospital. She stared a little dazedly at her reflection in the mirror over the washbasin.

Her deep-set eyes were dark with pain in a face drained of color. When she lifted her hand from her cheek, she could see again the reddened, hand-shaped impression on it. A trace of dried blood showed at the side of her mouth, a cut that must have been made by a ring Luigi wore on the hand that slapped her.

She tried to wipe from her mind what she had seen outside, but she couldn't figure out why she'd reacted that way to the crash. It hadn't all been because of her fear for Gino, she had to admit to herself.

Her reaction—the flashback and the hysteria—hadn't been caused by her fear for Gino. No, it was when she'd found that the man injured was Shane Jaeger that it had happened. Anxiety clutched at her stomach now as she wondered about his condition. He'd looked so deathly still as the emergency crew extricated him from the wreckage, carrying him away on the stretcher to somewhere within this building. Few men had ever had the impact on her that this man had from the first time they'd met. The thought that he might have died from the crash had a disturbing effect on her and she couldn't stop trembling.

A door opened behind her. A smiling nurse took her pulse and temperature, casting a concerned glance at her bruised cheek. Jaclyn was told that the doctor would be in to see her as soon as he had attended to Mr. Jaeger.

"How—" Jaclyn began, but the woman was gone, moving out the door in a swift white blur. Could Shane have survived that awful, flaming crash? she asked herself.

"So, how are you feeling, young lady?" the doctor asked her, touching the injured side of her face with careful, professional hands as the nurse brought a tray of first aid supplies to his side.

"My cheek hurts a little," she admitted. "But I didn't really need to bother you with it. I have to be getting back outside. You see, I'm covering this race for a magazine, and I can't miss anything."

But the doctor had noticed her trembling, and now inclined his head and watched her, unnerving her slightly with his scrutiny.

"Just what happened?" he asked. She avoided his eyes and mumbled something about getting in someone's way.

He swabbed the cut with something that smelled antiseptic and stung. "That's not what I was told." His words were quiet, but it was clear that he wouldn't be put off by her obvious fib.

Then she remembered the mark that showed bright against the pallor of her face, almost as if someone had dipped their hand in paint and put it to her cheek.

"We were told," he continued, "by the young man who brought you here, that he'd had to slap your face. He said you were hysterical after the accident, and he was more concerned about that than with the cut on your cheek."

She sighed and decided to tell the truth. There was no need to look at their faces. There would be that familiar look of pity.

"Are you sure you don't want to return to your hotel?" the doctor questioned. When Jaclyn shook her head forcefully he shrugged and finished tending to her cheek. "That should do it. There won't be a scar," he told her, and turned to leave.

"Doctor?"

"Yes?" He turned back to her, a slight frown on his face, evidence of his disapproval that she wouldn't take his advice.

"How—I mean, is Mr. Jaeger alive?" She had to know.

His frown cleared. "Of course. He was knocked unconscious, and he's suffering from a concussion. But he's awake now, and I think he'll be okay. We'll be moving him over to the local hospital for a few days." He nodded at her thanks, evidently seeing nothing unusual in her request for information about the actor, and left.

Jaclyn looked up to see the nurse watching her. "Is something wrong?"

A flush crept up into the nurse's plump cheeks. "No. Well, yes," she admitted. "Don't I recognize you? I'm not sure how I know your face, though."

Now it was Jaclyn's turn to blush. "A picture of me was in the evening paper the other day. It appears everyone has seen it." She walked over to the mirror and stared at herself, sighing. She tried a touch of makeup to conceal the rapidly darkening bruise, then powder. But nothing worked. Finally she combed a wave of her hair down one side so that it covered as much of her cheek as possible.

"Now you look like that famous movie actress of the forties. I think her name was Veronica Lake," the nurse noted as she watched Jaclyn. "You know, that cheek is going to look pretty bruised tomorrow."

"It looks as if I've been in a fight." Jaclyn grimaced.

The nurse picked up the tray of used supplies, telling Jaclyn to wait and she would show her out. But certain that she could find her way, Jaclyn walked out. To her chagrin she realized that she had been too upset when she and Luigi had entered the building to notice which direction they had come from. Luigi had gone back to the pit area, and now the nurse was nowhere to be seen. Finally Jaclyn started down the long corridor. Voices were coming from a room at the end. She found her steps slowing as she heard Shane's name mentioned.

"I mean it, Shane! Just what did you expect?" a Gallic voice chided in a friendly tone. "You were tempting fate just a little too much, eh?" The voice grew louder as the person approached the door. Jaclyn quickened her pace, not anxious to have the man open the door and think she had been eavesdropping as she passed.

The man stepped out quickly, and they nearly collided. For a sickening moment Jaclyn thought she had run into Shane as she looked up at the cobalt blue uniform and saw a dark-haired man looming above her.

But it was Alain, Shane's French co-driver. The crash helmet he held under one arm had a nasty dent plainly showing on it. It was a mute reminder of the wreck. The helmet had sustained a terrible blow to make the hard, protective surface dent in as it had.

"Is he really going to be all right?" Jaclyn had difficulty dragging her eyes from the headgear to stare into Alain's curious eyes.

The racer smiled. "He will be fine. He has a very hard head, that one, although I would not like to have him hear me saying that," Alain joked. But then his face grew sober. "He was very lucky. He will only have to rest for a few days." His words, softly spoken in French-accented English, were reassuring.

"Who are you whispering with out there, Alain?" Shane's voice rang out.

Alain smiled mischievously. He grasped Jaclyn by the elbow, drawing her inside the room. Nothing she could do slowed her relentless entry into the room.

"Just your Miss Taylor, Shane," he replied.

Jaclyn shot him a look of dismay. What had Shane been telling him? she wondered. Her eyes went to Shane, lying in the hospital bed. The sight of him frightened her. His face looked bloodless, almost vulnerable beneath the white bandages that swathed the upper portion of his head. Strands of his black hair fell over the bandages, which were wrapped lower over one side of his forehead, so that the corner of one eye was concealed, making him look darkly piratical. He raised his head, and she saw the familiar, burning contempt in his eyes, darkened with pain.

"So it's you!" he said. "Come in here and tell me what the newshound is asking, Alain," he ordered brusquely. His face contorted with a grimace of pain, and he was forced to lie back on the pillows again. For a moment he looked even paler than he had when she'd entered the room.

Jaclyn colored at his words, and cast Alain an embarrassed glance. But he grasped her arm more firmly and propelled her toward Shane's bed. Now that she was closer, she could see the beads of perspiration that had broken out on his upper lip from the pain his movement had caused. There were white lines around his colorless mouth. His lashes made dark shadows on his lean cheeks as he kept his eyes closed for a moment. The accident, after a lengthy, grueling race, had taken its toll.

"Just what were you doing nosing about in the hallway?" he demanded in icy fury. "Were you trying to get a big 'scoop' for your magazine, Brenda Starr?"

"No! It wasn't like that at all, really!" she protested. She backed away at his harsh words, trying frantically to pull away from Alain's grasp. The wave of hair that covered her bruised cheek swung away as she moved. She heard the Frenchman utter a sound of surprise.

"Mon Dieu!" Alain exclaimed. His grip tightened. He tilted her chin up with a gentle hand, gazing with concern at her cheek. "What happened to your face?"

"N-nothing," she stuttered, aware of the curious stares of the two men. With a strength born of the fear that Shane would continue to taunt her, she pulled away from Alain and fled from the room.

"Jaclyn, what's goin' on?" Mitch stood in the doorway. "Wait," he called as she pushed past him and rushed from the building.

Outside, the cars were moving swiftly, green lights replacing the caution ones. The wreckage of Shane's car had been towed away. It was as if nothing had happened.

She made her way back to the pits to sit, somewhat subdued, and watch the last hour of the race. The end of the race was an anticlimax for her. The American team that had led the race came in first, a British one second. Gino and Sophia had finished fifth place. Shane and Alain were listed as tenth. The accident had reduced Gino's rival to a still-respectable place in the field, because it had happened so late in the race. In a strange twist of fate, Gino had triumphed over his rival. But Jaclyn knew that it wouldn't afford Gino any satisfaction. He would always

107

wonder if Shane would have bested him if the crash hadn't happened.

The winners were in victory lane, where their words with the announcer interviewing them were carried over the speedway public-address system. They held aloft their trophies and accepted kisses from beauty queens.

But as Sophia stood in the pits and answered questions from the knot of reporters surrounding her, Jaclyn could see that she was very happy to be where she was. At least this time! Brother and sister hugged each other as cameras caught the scene, and the drivers accepted the congratulations of crew, fans, and press. Jaclyn smiled as she sat in the shadows of the pits, watching as her friends reviewed the race for their listeners. Finally Sophia raised an imperious hand and stopped the questioning, a worried look on her face.

"Has anyone heard how Signor Jaeger is?" she wanted to know. Only when she was reassured that his condition was not serious did she agree to answer a few more questions.

Gradually the fans filtered out of the grandstands and the infield. Some wore happy expressions, evidence that their favorite team or car had finished well, and all appeared to have had a good time. Well-wishers filtered slowly out of victory lane and the pits. Perhaps if there had been more people around, Jaclyn wouldn't have been able to see so clearly the handsome man being pushed past in his wheelchair. And know his identity.

She draws even now, this metal mistress. She still lures him with her siren song to a place such as this, when she has had her hand in maiming his body, Jaclyn thought to herself almost despairingly. Yet the man, a former racer paralyzed from a crash, appeared to be enjoying his return to a familiar scene with less mental pain than she had been experiencing, she had to admit.

The mass of shifting humanity tumbled through the exits as the announcer gave finishing statistics. The cars that completed the race had driven a distance approximating the mileage to the other side of the country; had broken old records and set new ones. Drivers had taken home a large prize purse with new sponsorship of the race by a soft-drink company.

The mood of the place downshifted as it became nearly deserted now. The emptying speedway seemed almost bereft, as its purpose was fulfilled for another race day. Jaclyn found herself becoming a little gloomy as the day darkened and she waited for a ride back to the hotel with the tired Spinnellis. The golden thrill of the afternoon was passing, leaving the same hard work that had preceded the race for those crews and drivers as they packed up to leave.

Jaclyn saw some drivers so exhausted that they sat, slumped with fatigue, wasted gladiators from the automotive arena of combat. Yet other drivers, adrenaline still pumping, had trouble unwinding. One driver was good-naturedly being told to "go take another lap around the track, but without your car this time" by a crew member.

Bits and pieces of litter lay on the ground, skittering aimlessly about in the fitful gusts of cooling dusk winds that carried the strong smell of racing fuel and rubber. A wadded-up scrap of newspaper rolled toward Jaclyn in a brisk path, like a tumbleweed with a preordained course, lodging against her foot. She found herself bending to pick it up and smooth it out on her knee. Her eyes widened with surprise as the creased paper image of a confident, handsome Shane Jaeger smiled up at her. Unexpected tears burned at the back of her eyelids. She rubbed at them with one hand, screwing the paper up and throwing it away.

"Well, *cara,* are you going to congratulate me?"

Gino stood before her, the collar of his scarlet uniform unzipped carelessly for comfort now that the race was over, running a hand through his hair in a tired gesture. Sophia came over to join them, and the two were a study in happy exhaustion.

"I was waiting to congratulate you. I thought I'd never get a chance to get you two alone. You both did a marvelous job!" she said with warmth.

Gino frowned slightly, as if he were surprised that she didn't have more enthusiasm. But before he could speak someone called him away.

Sophia stared at her friend, obviously puzzled, too. She pulled up a folding chair next to Jaclyn and sat down. "Is something wrong, Jaclyn?"

"No, why?" She tried to appear nonchalant.

Sophia shook her head and continued to look perplexed. "You're so—quiet." Then she groaned as she, too, was interrupted.

But the crew member who interrupted was Luigi, who wanted Jaclyn, not Sophia. He apologized for having to leave her at the infield hospital so that he could get back to the race.

Jaclyn thanked him for his help, secretly sorry that he had come over to ask about her while she and Sophia sat together. The Italian woman's eyes widened with curiosity as Jaclyn felt a cool hand turn her face up, so that the remaining light played on the darkening bruise, and she was forced to stare into Sophia's sympathetic eyes. Sophia

110

turned and thanked Luigi, too, for watching over Jaclyn, and he left.

"Oh, Jaclyn, I guess it wasn't such a good idea for you to come to this race, was it?" she asked sadly.

"I'm all right, really," Jaclyn sought to reassure her. "It looks worse than it is."

"But the pain is more than skin-deep," Sophia said in a quiet voice. "It opened old wounds inside, didn't it?"

Jaclyn shrugged. "Who could have known what would happen? I never dreamed I'd get hysterical like that. I'd gotten over the nightmares. I was beginning to get interested again in racing. I *wanted* to come."

"Did you think it was Gino in the crash?"

"At first. But then even when I saw it wasn't, it—didn't matter." She frowned and shook her head slowly. "I can't figure it out exactly."

Sophia inclined her head to one side, studying Jaclyn's face. "I wonder if it is all because of what happened before? Or was it something else, too? *Someone* else?"

Jaclyn's head jerked up at Sophia's words, surprise registering on her face. Those were the same questions she had been asking herself. Why? Could the impact of Shane's personality have been so strong that he had penetrated the defenses she'd built around herself, to protect her from hurt?

Or was it guilt she felt that his accident had happened so soon after she had thought that if Shane crashed, she would have an easy way out of the interview? She became aware that Sophia was watching the play of expressions on her face. Sophia wore a smile that only a true Italian could wear, one of understanding those who loved.

"It happens to all of us one day, does it not, Jaclyn?"

111

"But I'm not in love with Gino." Jaclyn pretended to misunderstand.

"Come, now, we haven't been talking about Gino," Sophia chided her gently.

Jaclyn stared at her shoes. "No, I'm not going to admit that I'm in love with Shane Jaeger. I can't be. No! I *won't* be."

"Why not?"

Jaclyn got to her feet and paced before Sophia. "He races, remember? And he's arrogant and hateful and—and—"

"And you love him." Sophia smiled.

Jaclyn stopped suddenly, her face a study in conflicting emotions. "Yes," she said softly. "Yes."

Later, back at the hotel, Jaclyn sank down gratefully on her bed. It had been a long twenty-four hours. But more than that, an emotionally exhausting time. She closed her eyes and tried to nap. But the roar of car engines seemed to linger in her ears, and with it, the memories of the day.

That night, she had a last, quiet meal with Sophia and Gino. They would be leaving the next day with their crew. Jaclyn knew a peculiar loneliness at losing friends she had become close to once again. She'd miss them even more after this past week, when they had come together again as adults.

Gino was pensive as they toasted each other's continuing success in their separate worlds. Jaclyn sensed he regretted that they hadn't become more than friends. Sophia was relaxed and at ease, although still very tired after a brief rest. She spoke for all of them when she said they'd be glad to get more sleep that night.

They talked and reflected on the race, drinking wine at a table overlooking the night-darkened ocean, until at last

112

they had to give in to fatigue and go to their rooms. Finally, despite all the excitement of the past twenty-four hours, Jaclyn slept, exhausted.

Promising to send Sophia and Gino a copy of the magazine article when it was published, Jaclyn saw her friends off at the airport the next day. She and Sophia hugged like sisters, and if Gino's kiss was a little more than brotherly —well, what of it? she asked herself. He was leaving, and it might be years before they would meet again.

It was a little lonely afterward in the hotel, and a little hard for Jaclyn to get down to work.

Perhaps what I need is a walk on the beach before I settle down, she told herself. She needed to go over in her mind what she wanted to convey to her readers about Sophia. A good sea breeze might blow the tiredness from her mind, and an hour's ramble along the shoreline would get her into a better mood for writing.

Most of the race crowd had left town. In the lull, the beach appeared nearly deserted, almost for her alone to walk along and enjoy. She could see why Shane Jaeger loved it here at this time of the year. Shane, Shane. She had to stop thinking about him. The paper had said yesterday that he was doing well. But he remained in the hospital, and on her mind.

She turned her attention back to the article she was writing, as much to forget Shane as to get down to work. It was always a little hard to get started. But then, when the words began to come, she would rush to her typewriter. There, she had no trouble, words flowing from her mind through her fingers onto the typewriter keys. When she had a rough draft, an essence of the person she was writing about, whether it took several hours or nearly all day and night, she'd collapse and sleep, later going over what she'd written when she awoke.

It might be hard this time, she thought, to write about a friend, and stay impartial. But she had become very fond of several other people, once strangers, she had interviewed, and she'd had no trouble with those articles.

An elderly couple strolled toward her, arm in arm, enjoying quiet companionship. There were few visitors to the beach today, fewer still in the cool water. A car would occasionally make a slow tour of the beach.

The sun warmed her as she walked. Thinking of Sophia's childhood, it came to her that she should start with her remembrance of Sophia learning to drive, sitting on her father's lap, in Italy, when she was a child. She didn't often start an interview this way. Sometimes the important events of a person's life began at twenty, forty, any age. But Sophia's hadn't. Her motivation to drive had started so early, and suddenly Jaclyn turned back toward the hotel. She had the start of her article.

The desk clerk smiled at Jaclyn when she stopped for her key. It was pleasant to have a break between groups of visitors to the hotel, she told Jaclyn. The next tourist wave would be the college students from all around the country, down for relaxation and a quick suntan on their Spring break. Then the hotel would be lively again, she said, plainly showing her enjoyment at meeting the people who moved through the motel, changeable as the seasons in which they came.

Some people approached the desk, and Jaclyn turned away to go to her room, picking up a complimentary copy of the newspaper on the reception desk. Inside the elevator, riding upstairs to her room, she opened it and was startled to see Shane Jaeger's face leap up at her from the

114

page. Jaeger, pictured sitting up in bed, would be leaving the hospital soon, the accompanying article reported. He was still suffering from "wicked" headaches, caused by the concussion, but was restless to get out.

The elevator doors slid open, and Jaclyn stepped out, absorbed in the paper, and walked slowly down the corridor to her room. What were his plans? the reporter had asked—a person Jaclyn remembered Shane didn't hold in contempt, as he did other members of the press. Jaeger's face had brightened, the reporter noted, as the actor mysteriously told of plans to "settle a score." Those were his very words, the newswriter said. But he hadn't been able to get the actor to explain the meaning behind his enigmatic statement.

Jaclyn nearly dropped the newspaper. *Score to settle.* He couldn't mean—no, he didn't mean her! *Did* he? The challenge he'd thrown at her, when he'd dared her to interview him and not mangle the truth—surely he didn't *really* mean to hold her to it?

She let herself into her room, absently dropping the newspaper on the bed as she went to stare out the window. Should she cut short her stay, just in case he meant her? She reached for the telephone, deciding to try to change her plane reservation. Chicken, her conscience called her, but she ignored it.

But even before her fingers touched the receiver, the telephone rang, and she jumped. Her hand flew to her mouth. Suddenly she had an awful premonition of whose voice would be on the other end of the line. It rang, and rang again, and finally she had to pick it up.

"Jaclyn?" a familiar, mocking voice asked. There was no need for the man to identify himself, she thought with a sinking feeling in the pit of her stomach.

115

"I thought so," she muttered.

"What?" came the sharp rejoinder.

"Nothing." There was a pause. "What did you want, Mr. Jaeger?"

"You, Jaclyn."

"Me?" she gasped in surprise.

"Yes, you," he went on relentlessly. "I gather that you've read the afternoon paper."

"How—how did you know?" It came out as a croak.

He laughed. "By the rather frightened way you answered the telephone."

"I'm not frightened of you," she told him defiantly.

"You should be." His voice was low and menacing. "You didn't forget our little agreement?"

"Yes, I did, as a matter of fact." She tried to sound casual. "And since you're injured, it'll suit both of us if we forget it, won't it?" She crossed her fingers.

"No way, Jaclyn," he said harshly. "And I won't listen to any excuses. I mean to make you pay for that remark at the party. And my having a few headaches from this blasted concussion isn't going to save you from your part of the deal. I'm going to show you and all the others once and for all that no matter how I treat you people, you'll still maliciously print whatever you please."

"But—" she began, but was cut off.

"I'll be leaving the hospital in the morning. Be ready in front of your hotel at nine o'clock, and we'll go to my place."

"But I don't want to interview you at your home," she said hurriedly. "Can't we do it somewhere else?" She didn't relish the thought of being alone with him, not when she remembered what had happened on the nearly deserted beach that one morning.

116

His laugh was sardonic. "And just where do you propose? If we went anywhere and I was recognized, we wouldn't be able to talk. My housekeeper will be there to chaperon, if you're worried about your reputation."

She must have let out a relieved sigh, for he laughed sardonically.

"Be ready," he said brusquely. "I don't want to have to come up after you."

"Now wait a minute—" she began, anger flaring within her. No one was going to threaten her! But he'd hung up!

She slammed the receiver down and flung herself on the bed. Damn the man, she fumed. How was she going to get out of this?

It's strange, she thought to herself. She'd been so worried about him that day he'd crashed. And she'd admitted to Sophia that she had fallen in love with him. Since then she'd tried to forget about him, telling herself that she must be one of undoubted dozens who had harbored an infatuation for him. She'd been successful, up to now, in not thinking about him. Hah! Don't lie to yourself, her conscience laughed at her.

The sound of his voice had brought everything back— the clash of wills, the sparring with taunts and threats. There was something utterly ruthless about the man. He had a way of making others do what he wanted. She'd heard rumors he was a dictator on the film set. But she hadn't seen anything of that kind of behavior at the speedway, she had to admit. There he exercised control, but with persuasiveness, convincing others that he was right.

Why does he have to be so autocratic and iron-willed with me? she asked herself. Why does he keep insisting on this interview, even when he's not feeling well? She fumed and fumed, calming down only when she realized that there was nothing she could do about it. She hadn't thought of anything in days past. The inevitable had happened, and she might as well face it and get it over with.

He was right about one thing. She *was* a little afraid of him. It wasn't just that he had backed her into a corner, or that he had the power to make things uncomfortable. She was a little worried about interviewing someone with the kind of incredible popularity he had, and frightened that she might reveal unconsciously her feelings for him. What would he do with that knowledge?

Jaeger had been right when he'd said she would have no trouble selling an interview about him. Already she had received several telephone messages from magazine editors who had seen it reported that he was giving her an exclusive interview. The man had such a mystique about him that an interview in any magazine would draw readers. She could pick and choose any publication she wanted, name any price. But she didn't want to do it!

Her anger returned. Why had he picked on her, anyway? Darn him and his odious theories about the press being privacy intruders, gossipmongers.

Gossipmongers? Why did that word linger in her mind? It brought with it the unpleasant smell of unkind slander dredged up to feed the appetites of people who believed others deserved no privacy, no decency. Yet the low-minded and uneducated weren't the only people who enjoyed gossip. Nearly everyone wanted to believe a rumor about this or that person now and then.

Jaclyn drummed her fingers on the bedspread, thinking hard. And then her eyes lit up. That was it! She knew the way to make Shane Jaeger wish he hadn't forced her into this whole thing. She'd interview him all right. But when he asked her where the article would appear, she would stall until it was finished. And then he'd be in for a surprise!

She sat up and looked at herself in the mirror. There was a delicious gleam of excitement in her eyes as she picked up the telephone, dialed New York City, and asked for the number of a certain scandal magazine.

CHAPTER SIX

Promptly at nine the next morning, Jaclyn stood waiting outside the hotel. A sleek burgundy sports car pulled up. The driver reached across, pushed open the door, and impatiently waved his hand for her to enter.

"Get in, Jaclyn."

Jaclyn moved toward the car, frowning. Who had Jaeger sent for her?

It was Jaeger himself, his identity nearly concealed by sunglasses and a Stetson, like Mitch wore, pulled low over his forehead.

"Are you supposed to be driving?"

"Get in before we're seen," he commanded.

She got in.

"I knew you'd be waiting," he said with a chuckle. "What's the matter, afraid to drive with me?"

Jaclyn squeezed herself against the door, as far away from him as possible. She tossed her hair back and glared at him. So, he was launching the attack again, before saying as much as a simple hello! she thought. Darn the man!

"I think you *wanted* me to back out!" she returned.

She found herself clutching her big zippered writing

case to her chest as he turned his head and ran his eyes over her, smiling in a derisive way.

The car shot forward, and as they left the sheltered overhang of the hotel, sunlight filled the interior. It was then that she saw how haggard he looked. The healthy tan he'd had just days earlier was gone. He seemed less spirited than his tone had implied, and Jaclyn wondered if he was really well enough to be going home, much less be interviewed.

"Are you feeling all right?" she asked, concerned.

She should have known better. A dark eyebrow went up, and he smiled cynically.

"I only got a bump on the head," he said, scorning her sympathy.

"Have it your way." She shrugged her shoulders and turned her head to stare out the window. "I understood it was more than a bump. I thought you might not be up to doing an interview yet."

"Ah, but what could be more relaxing and enjoyable than sitting and talking with a beautiful woman?" His tone mocked the compliment of his words.

"Don't patronize me!" she snapped. She turned to face him, her eyes flashing in anger.

"I'm patronizing you by saying you're beautiful? Must be reverse vanity."

"I don't need your pseudocompliments, that's all," she told Shane in a slightly aggrieved tone. "Not when you act as if my only purpose is to sit around looking decorative or something, instead of doing my job."

Shane laughed, but it was a dry, humorless sound. "Don't worry, Jaclyn. I intend that we learn a lot about each other during the next week or two."

Jaclyn stiffened. "This is to be a one-sided interview,"

she informed him. "I don't make it a habit to exchange confidences about myself with the person I'm interviewing."

He shrugged, as if to tell her that her words were unimportant. "Call me Shane, *Jaclyn*. I thought you understood that *I'll* be the one who lays the ground rules here. I'll tell *you* what to expect from this arrangement. Ah, here we are," he concluded smoothly, before she could protest.

Jaclyn looked out the window as the car pulled into the driveway. "This is your house?" she asked in surprise.

"My home," he corrected.

It was an A-frame structure built of weathered wood that resembled sun- and salt-washed driftwood and buff-colored coquina rock. The house had a commanding view of the ocean, yet it had an air of privacy on the high dunes covered with waving sea oats.

"Disappointed?"

"No, not at all." She was enchanted with it, yet a little reluctant to tell him. "I guess I *was* expecting you to have something a little bit bigger, though, a little more . . ." She searched for an appropriate word.

"Ostentatious?" he inserted dryly.

She flushed.

They were met at the door by a plump, middle-aged woman who beamed a warm smile of welcome for Shane.

"Shane, I'm so happy to see you back home," she bubbled, giving him a motherly hug. Shane looked slightly embarrassed at the show of affection.

"Now, Katie," he groaned good-naturedly. "You'd think I'd been away longer than a couple of days."

"Well, you could have been killed." The woman sniffed,

quickly bending her head to search in her apron pockets for a tissue. "When I saw—"

"Enough," he said sternly. "Here, I want you to meet someone."

"Goodness, my manners!" the woman apologized. She looked at Jaclyn with interest. "So *you're* the one who's going to interview Shane. Now I can see why the old hermit changed his mind about press people."

"Enough, Katie. You keep forgetting who's boss around here," Shane said, smiling. "Anyway, Jaclyn's just warned me that I'm not to compliment her. Everything is to be strictly business."

"Yes, sir." Katie tried to look serious, but Jaclyn saw a gleam of mischief in the woman's eyes.

Shane motioned Jaclyn to precede him into the living room.

She thinks it's a joke—that Shane has me here to flirt with or something, she thought angrily, her face flaming with color.

Yet she forgot her anger the moment she entered the living room, the focal point of which was a huge glass window through which the crystal-green ocean seemed almost to enter the room. The furnishings and colors were downplayed to encompass the full beauty of the Atlantic. Soft beige carpeting the color of sand, glass shelves filled with sea objects and shells, and a sofa placed so that one could sit and look at the sea all captured the restful quality outside.

Shane's voice brought Jaclyn back to earth.

"What?"

"I asked if you were satisfied." His question was sardonic.

"Mmm," she murmured. "It's a beautiful room. And house, too."

He invited her to sit down. She chose a corner of the sofa as far from him as possible, to his obvious amusement.

"What are you learning about me from my environment?" he wanted to know. "It wasn't what you expected, was it?"

"Why do you say that?" she countered.

He put his feet up on the weathered wooden coffee table, slipped off his hat and dark glasses, and studied her, silver-gray eyes intent. "I'll bet you were expecting something different. A silken harem setting, perhaps, befitting my supposed reputation." He leaned toward her, leering like a silent-screen Valentino, enjoying her surprised reaction. "Or perhaps you thought I'd have a rough-and-ready ranch house reminiscent of my Western films? I recall you once accused me of being macho."

Jaclyn ignored him and began to take her things from her carryall. "I hadn't thought about it," she lied.

"What's that for?" he asked sharply as she bent to place her tape recorder on the table.

She looked up in surprise. "I use this for all my interviews."

"Why?"

"It helps," she began in a patient voice, "to enhance my notes, to record nuances of the person's speech, all sorts of things." She'd had to explain it to people slightly skittish of such devices before, but thought he'd be accustomed to it. "And," she added, not without a touch of malice, "it protects me from people who might try to say I misquoted them."

He rubbed his cheek with the knuckles of one hand.

"Ahh." He grinned. "Now we have the real reason. At least with me, right?"

"Yes. But if you object, we can always forget the whole thing," she added with a sweet smile, and bent to pick up the recorder from the table.

"That's fine."

She nearly dropped it. "What?"

"I said it's okay. What's the matter?"

"N-nothing," she stammered.

He chuckled. "You expected a fight, didn't you?"

"I don't know what to expect from you!" she shot back.

"But why shouldn't I agree? This way you'll have to tell the truth."

"I do anyway! This just makes sure *you* do, too." She shoved in a tape and slammed the lid down. "Now," she said icily, pencil poised above her notepad, "if you're ready."

"I thought you two might like some coffee before you start." Katie bustled into the room with a laden tray and placed it on the table before them. Apparently oblivious of the slight tension in the air, she chattered away about being glad to see Shane home again as she poured the coffee. "Will you have a piece of coffee cake, Miss Taylor?"

Jaclyn shook her head. "No, thanks. I had a large breakfast," she fibbed. She hadn't. Her stomach had churned too much at the thought of meeting Shane again, and coming here to his home to interview him.

The housekeeper fussed like a mother hen when Shane, too, refused a slice. "You've lost weight. Didn't they feed you at that place?" she clucked, shaking her head as she spoke. "You're pale, too. Are you sure you shouldn't be upstairs, in bed?"

"Sounds like a good idea, doesn't it, Jaclyn?" Shane asked, a mischievous glint in his eyes.

Jaclyn blushed hotly.

"Now, Shane, don't tease the young lady," the housekeeper reproved. "What if she starts thinking you're a flirt?"

Jaclyn choked on a mouthful of coffee.

"See, Katie? She really thinks a whole lot worse of me." Shane laughed as Jaclyn glared at him.

"Well, I'll leave you two to get on with that interview business. I'll be in the kitchen if you need me."

"Why does she have to make it sound like something is going on?" Jaclyn demanded in exasperation when the woman had left the room. "What does she think we're doing, besides working?"

"I wonder," Shane replied, unconcerned. His hand caressed her arm, traveled up it to stroke the softness of her cheek.

"I'm here for business, not pleasure. If either you or Katie has any trouble with that idea, I'll go right now," she retorted, moving away from his hand, secretly hating to do so.

"What a shame we can't combine business with pleasure," he mused. "Now, now, don't get alarmed," he chided as she sat up straighter. "I was just teasing."

She stared down at her coffee, growing cold in the cup, hoping he hadn't seen the fear that leaped in her eyes. His touch had sent a shiver of pleasure coursing through her. The only way she would get through this was to keep as much space between them as possible. If he ever guessed how she really felt about him, had felt that day when he had crashed . . .

"What?" She came to attention, realizing that he was talking to her.

"I said I'm ready to start, if you are. Are you okay?"

"Fine," she said quickly. "But it's you I should be asking about. Are you sure that this won't be too much for you? After all, you just got out of the hospital."

"All this fuss over a bump on the head. I'll be fine. Now," he said, leaning back against the cushions, "I hope you won't start out asking if I sleep in the nude."

"It's the very last question I'd ask, I assure you," she replied tartly, reaching for her notepad. "First, why did you want this interview?" she asked point-blank.

His expression remained bland. "You know why."

"I know that you have a big grudge against the press, that you have a need to pick on me. But let's get your side for the readers."

He pressed the tips of his fingers together and stared at her over them, studying her until she squirmed and tugged her skirt down over her knees.

"Why did I choose you?" he asked aloud, thinking it over. "Was it the way we got along so well every time we met? Because we respected each other? Because I knew you'd make me look good in print?"

"Oh, forget it!" she snapped. "I shouldn't have asked." Throwing her notepad down, she jumped to her feet and crossed the room to stand before the window. She counted to ten, drew a deep breath, then turned to him.

"I don't know why you're playing this cat-and-mouse game with me. It's just not going to work. I knew it wouldn't from the start. I won't have you playing games with me. I've got better things to do." She pushed her hair back from her face in an angry gesture and stood, hands on hips, defiantly waiting for him to answer.

"I apologize."

"What?"

"I said I'm sorry. It was just too irresistible. I had to tease you. I promise to be on my best behavior from now on, okay?"

Her eyes narrowed into slits of suspicion. "I just don't know why you had to persist in this notion of an interview, anyway. I said I wouldn't be a whipping boy for the things the press has supposedly done to you."

"I think one of these days you'll figure out why I insisted." His expression was enigmatic.

"What's that supposed to mean?"

"Never mind for now. Come sit down again."

She walked back to the sofa and sat, stiffly.

"Did I tell you what I've learned about you?"

Her hand flew to her throat. "W-what?"

"Maybe he didn't dig deep enough." Shane frowned. "Tell me, do you have a criminal record or something to account for the fear I just saw in your eyes?"

"No, no, of course not. You just startled me, the way you spoke, that's all." She picked up her notepad with a hand that trembled.

"I'd say there was more than that. But then you've always been a mystery to me."

"There isn't anything mysterious about me," she denied. "What was it you were going to tell me?"

"My agent checked into your background."

"For what?" Her words came out a little more sharply than she would have wished. She could have kicked herself when she saw the alert look on his face.

"I wanted to know what you'd written. You've done quite well for yourself, interviewed some important people, haven't you?"

"Yes, I guess so." She tried not to let out a sigh of relief.

"And for some of the better magazines. Which magazine will this interview appear in?"

"I—I don't know yet," she lied. "You see, I'm a freelancer. I'll have to decide if I'll make it a personality piece, a Q and A, or something else before I offer it to a magazine."

"Explain."

"Why?" She was slightly puzzled by his change of mood.

"Because I'm interested in you. And in what you do."

"A personality piece means that I'll record the interview in a way that also makes note of things I learn about you—details and observations, anecdotes you tell, all sorts of things. A Q and A is the style used mostly in, say, *Playboy* magazine, where a summary or synopsis of the person's background is placed at the top, then straight questions and answers follow."

"What do you prefer?"

"The personality piece, I think. You can explore a person more in that style, and sketch the person's character with their actions and little details. Their human qualities, I guess I'm trying to say."

"Doesn't that make it harder for you to write? It sounds like a lot of work, too."

She shook her head. "Both take enormous work and time. But it's worth it. And speaking of time, we really should be starting."

"Are you ready for lunch, Shane?" Katie interrupted.

"Lunch? Already? The morning has gone quickly."

"Yes." Jaclyn sighed. "And I didn't even get to ask the first question." I certainly didn't manage this well, she chided herself.

"Miss Taylor is staying, isn't she?" the housekeeper asked.

"Of course," Shane said, refusing to listen to her protests. "We can start again after lunch if you like."

"Well . . ."

Shane was polite during the meal, but firmly refused to talk about anything personal. "I never discuss business when a beautiful woman dines with me."

She tilted her head to one side and studied him, frowning. "I'm losing ground here."

"But we have time to know each other, don't we?" he asked. His eyes were a warm woodsmoke-gray as he watched her over the rim of his glass, containing wine that Katie had fussed about him having when he was just home from the hospital.

A few minutes later as they were getting up from the table, Shane staggered a little and grasped the back of his chair for support.

"Are you ill?" she cried in alarm as he passed a shaky hand over his eyes.

"No, I'll be fine. I probably just got up too quickly. Maybe I drank too much wine."

"One glass? Don't be ridiculous. You've just overdone it, is what it is." She placed a hand on his arm. "Don't you think you should go to bed?"

"Will you tuek me in?" His mouth widened into a wicked grin.

"Oh, Katie, Shane wants to be tucked into bed," Jaclyn said brightly as she saw the housekeeper enter the room. She laughed at his scowl, and crossed the room to gather her things. "I'll come back in the morning if you like."

"I'd like," he said softly.

The next day, when they had settled down in the living

130

room again, Jaclyn vowed not to let him get away with his probing her as he had all morning. It's time, she told herself, to get this thing started, to let him know who's in charge of the interview. It was supposed to be the interviewer, not the interviewee.

But she wasn't altogether successful. And she couldn't exactly put her finger on why, either. Penetrating the aura of mystery around the man, and his obsessive desire for privacy, was proving difficult, she found.

"Why did you go into acting?"

"Because I'm good at it. And I wanted to see certain things done in films."

"Such as?"

"I wanted to probe the emotions of people, find out why they act as they do, tell an important or entertaining story. I have a project coming up that would better explain the way I feel about it," he added mysteriously.

"What is it?"

"I can't say now."

"What role was your favorite? And why?"

"Whatever I'm doing at the time is my favorite role. And I always hope that my next is my best."

"Do you have any trouble identifying with a character you're playing?"

"Acting isn't just identifying with a character," he corrected her. "It helps to identify, to understand what and why he is what he is, but then that's just the first step. The next is portraying him, however you feel he is like you in some small or large way."

"What character you've played is most like you? And least?"

He pushed a hand through his thick dark hair as he

131

thought. "I guess Michael Brown in *Yesterdays* was the closest to my personality. Why do you look so surprised?"

Jaclyn shook her head. "I guess it's because I don't exactly see you that way. Michael was . . ." She trailed off, trying to remember.

"Serious, introspective. *Loving,*" he filled in for her, with emphasis on the last word. "Why do you suppose you have trouble visualizing me as being like Michael?"

"I—I don't know. Perhaps because I don't really know you." She bent her head over her notepad, and thick curtains of her hair fell forward at each side of her face to hide her expression.

"Or because you find it easier to believe the worst of me."

"Why would I do that?" She looked up, startled.

"Because that way you can hide your true feelings about me."

She shifted uncomfortably. "I—" she began, then changed her mind. Better to ignore the remark and not get into a personal discussion. He was too near the truth, anyway. Something had clicked between them those first times they had met. Only after Shane had thought her to be hiding her profession had they sparred so. She'd thought of selling the interview to that gossip magazine in spite when he'd insisted she interview him. She still didn't understand why. . . .

"You were asking me what was the character least like me?" He brought her back to attention.

"Yes."

"I'm still not sure I carried off the role in *Nations.* The character was someone who becomes cynical, gives up on trying to change people's thinking about an issue he feels strongly about."

"You don't feel you're cynical?"

"Not really. Only about certain things."

"What about the press?"

He held his hands up. "Please, don't let's get on that again!" he said in mock terror.

"And what about this hiding out from the public? I noticed that you don't even have a telephone," she persisted.

"You don't understand, do you?" A muscle jerked in his cheek as he leaned forward. "I can't go anywhere without someone bothering me, asking for autographs, a chance for a part, all sorts of things. This is the only place I have a chance to really feel myself, to get away from the Hollywood rat race, the ego trip, the living in a goldfish bowl. And I gave up a telephone after I had to change my number every month, still wondering if the operators were listening in on my conversations."

"But you weren't bothered at the race," she argued.

"You weren't paying attention. A guard stood at the back of the pit space, and if I hadn't been injured, I'd have left wearing the fake beard, sunglasses, and hat I keep in my car. If I didn't enjoy my work so much, I'd give it all up because of that."

"What would you do if you didn't act?" she asked curiously.

"That's easy. I'd direct. I think every actor is a frustrated director. We'd all love to see if we couldn't do it better."

"You directed one of your films, didn't you?"

"Yes. I loved it, although it was hard work, directing the whole project while trying to concentrate on my part in it."

"Didn't your female co-star in the film call you a tyrant?"

His face darkened. "Yes."

"Why?"

"Because she wasn't paying attention to her work. And I expect the very best from everyone on the set, down to the last stagehand. It's no more than I expect from myself."

"What sort of actor do you consider yourself to be?"

"A good one."

"Isn't that a bit conceited?"

"Is it egotistical to think of yourself in honest terms? Are you a hack writer?"

"Of course not!" she snapped, stung.

"See my point?" he asked. Moving closer, he reached out a hand and touched her, gently massaging the spot between her eyebrows.

"What are you doing?"

"Relax," he soothed. "I'm just stroking away that funny little frown of yours. It appears whenever you concentrate or get angry."

"I didn't know I was getting angry so much." She smiled slightly and was a little sorry when he moved his hand. Her skin tingled from his touch.

"Not lately. But I could never figure out why you did so much before." His smile was mocking.

"Because you behave insufferably sometimes, you know that."

He laughed. "Only when you go too far with your questions."

"It's called the age of the tough interview now, didn't you know?" she shot back.

"I do now. Why, I need to rest up every afternoon after a session with you."

"If I'm overtiring you . . ." she began.

"Quite the contrary. I was just teasing you. What do you do in the afternoons, after you leave here?"

She looked out the window a little wistfully. "I've tried to spend some time on the beach after I've written up questions I need to ask you, and typed up notes and things."

"Stay longer, extend your vacation."

"I can't. I have to get back home soon."

"So little time," Jaclyn heard him mutter.

"What?"

"Nothing. Look, how about staying later each day? We could have lunch on the sun deck each day, stay out there for an hour or so," he offered.

"Could we?" She couldn't hide the eagerness in her voice. "Then I could get some sun."

"Sure." He smiled, his eyes warm on her.

True to his word, they lunched outdoors the next day, and after that. She found herself relaxing a little more with him, freer in the sun and air outside than when she was inside. There, even with Katie in the next room, cleaning or cooking, she felt in his "domain," his space. She studied him covertly as they ate. He could disarm her utterly when he wanted to be cooperative like this. Yet he couldn't diminish her feelings about him, his attraction, no matter how he acted. The more she was with him, the more she wanted to be; the more she learned about him, the more she wanted to know.

He looked up and caught her staring at him. "What's the matter?"

"I—noticed you looked a little tired," she said quickly. "Are you sure I should stay longer?"

"Thanks for telling me I look like I feel," he said sardonically. "I haven't been resting. Something's been on my mind lately."

"What?" It had sounded as if he said some*one* under his breath, after his last sentence.

He put his elbows on the table, rested his chin on his hands, and studied her for a long moment. Then he shook his head. "Nothing. I didn't say anything."

She was disconcerted.

"You asked earlier about the research I do for my parts, before Katie interrupted us for lunch."

"Yes." She fumbled for her things, spread them on the table, and turned on the recorder. "Go ahead."

He leaned back in his chair. "Well, the first step is obvious. I read the script. Then, if it's been adapted from a book, I read that, too, as well as anything written about the character, if it's available."

"I've read that you sometimes go to the locale where the character lived, or might have done."

"You know a lot about me, don't you?"

She blushed. "I dug up some material before I came down for the race."

"Why?"

"My editor thought I might have a chance to talk to you. He said I should know something about you."

"How prophetic. Too bad I didn't have the same opportunity with you."

"Why would you need that? I'm the one doing the interviewing." She was puzzled.

He shrugged. "Might have made things a little easier. Not as interesting, though."

"What are you talking about?" She wondered if they were conducting two entirely different conversations today.

"Didn't you bring something to sun in?"

"Are you changing the subject?" she asked suspiciously.

"Would I do that?" he countered. "I just thought you might like to change into it."

"I wore a halter top beneath my blouse." She looked down a bit uncertainly at her blouse, then unbuttoned it, revealing the halter. Made of crochet, the dark-green top's twisted strands made the most of her curves.

"Much better," he approved.

"I don't know how much more casual you want me to dress," she grumbled as she put her blouse aside.

"A bikini would be fine." He grinned.

She frowned. "I'm not here to have fun."

"Don't make it sound so much like work." He sounded a little piqued.

"I'm sorry. I didn't mean it that way. But even if we're talking like friends, it's still work for me to do the interviewing."

"Don't you know we can't ever be friends?"

"If you'd stop bearing grudges—" she began.

"That has nothing to do with it," he interrupted. "Don't jump to conclusions, Jaclyn." He reached across the table and stroked her bare arm. "Do you think a man and a woman can be friends?"

"Of—of course." His touch was distracting.

"Not *some* men and women."

She frowned. "What would you have them be?"

"Lovers," he said softly. His eyes mesmerized her.

Her breath caught in her throat. "I—I don't want to—"

"Where's the magic thread?" He changed the subject swiftly.

"Magic thread?"

"I mean, can I find the starter thread in this thing—

137

what's it called? Macrame, crochet, what? Will it all unravel for me?" His fingers touched the material where it tied around her neck.

She pulled away from his touch. "Stop that. Maybe I'd better put my blouse back on."

"No, my prim Jaclyn. I'll leave you alone," he said, smiling.

"Don't laugh at me!" Her back stiffened.

He pretended to look apologetic. "I won't. Anything is better than the way you came dressed that first day."

"What was wrong with it?"

"You looked so uptight and businesslike. And that color!" He sent his eyes heavenward. "I knew I was in for it the minute I saw you in that battle-flag-red dress!"

"It was scarlet," she corrected him dryly. "And I should be dressed for business, not as casually as you've talked me into dressing lately."

"Oh, relax, Jaclyn," he chided. "After all, I interrupted your vacation. At least don't make me feel guilty by coming here like that each day."

She laughed, a clear, high peal of merriment. "I can't imagine you feeling guilty for this whole thing."

He shrugged and turned his attention to the sea oats, which waved gently in the breeze. "Sometimes I think you want to believe the worst of me. It helps you hide your feelings, I guess."

"What on earth are you talking about?"

He stood, hands on hips, and stared beyond the dune grasses to the ocean. "I'm a man, Jaclyn. No better or worse just because of my profession. Neither saint nor sinner. Someone is always going to find something bad to say about me if it suits them. I can't help that. But I'd hoped you'd changed your opinion of me these past few days." He put his hands on her shoulders. "Look at me, Jaclyn. How do you really feel about me?" His words were spoken quietly but intensely as he stared into her eyes.

Confused, she shook her head. "I don't know. You've been—different lately. I don't know how to feel."

A breeze blew his thick black hair back from his forehead, exposing the thin white line of a scar. It was a vivid reminder of his accident, and Jaclyn shivered.

"What is it?"

"Nothing." She looked away.

His hands left her shoulders, yet he didn't move from his place before her. There was silence for a moment, then he asked, "How about a walk?"

"Are you sure you feel up to it?"

He groaned. "Don't tell me I have another woman nagging me."

"Katie only means well. She told me she doesn't think you're sleeping well, that you're working too hard on some project. And I—" She broke off as Shane's face darkened.

"You what?"

"Don't look so accusing!" she snapped. "I haven't been asking her about your private life. And she wouldn't tell me, anyway. You should know Katie only cares for you. She wouldn't hurt you for the world."

"No, she wouldn't," Shane said slowly. "Would you, Jaclyn?"

Jaclyn started. She stared up at him, trying not to look frightened. Had he guessed that she'd once wanted to sell the interview to that scandal magazine?

"What do you mean?"

He sighed. "Nothing. Theoretical question. I don't know why I asked. How about that walk?"

She got to her feet. Shane said something about sunglasses and went inside. When he returned he drew on the glasses, hiding his identity.

"Is that why you aren't recognized here?" Shane took her hand to help her down the dunes, and then casually retained it.

He nodded. "Partly, I guess. It's also because no one really expects me to be here, except during those few days of the race. The few people who have given me a second look have obviously decided I look like that actor, what's-his-name."

They walked along the shoreline, savoring the quiet beauty of the beach. Shane bent to pick up a pearly smooth chunk of abalone that had washed up on shore, and a delicate, creamy white shell, its outer lip touched with pale pink.

"This shell reminds me of you," he told her.

"Me? How?"

"You're like the sensitive little animal that hides in a shell. You try to hide your feelings from me with layer upon layer of shell, just like this creature did. But I'm finding ways to break down your reserve, wear a hole in that beautiful hard shell you've built around yourself."

The sea breeze spun a golden veil of hair around Jaclyn's face, hiding her expression for a moment. "Maybe that's true," she said slowly. "But if you destroy that shell you think I have around me, you may hurt me. That little creature died, remember."

Shane reached out a hand and smoothed her hair back so that he could see her face. He shook his head. "No, it won't hurt, I promise. I wouldn't hurt you, Jaclyn." *Trust me,* his eyes seemed to say.

She shook her head doubtfully, staring down at the water swirling around their bare feet.

"You know, I don't understand it," Shane said, frowning. He seemed moody, reflective today.

"What?"

He looked at her. "All this fuss people make about me, about actors. Why is the public so interested in what I think, what I say? Look at my footprint," he directed, lifting one of his feet. It had filled with the seawater, and now its impression was being wiped away with the receding wave. "Don't you see? I'm just like that. Whatever impression I make in this world is just as transitory, just as temporary. Even if I make a good film, is it any more lasting a contribution than what any other man does?"

"I think so," she said slowly. "It lasts, just as a good book does, or a painting—any creative effort."

"So you think we all make some sort of dent on this old planet?" His tone was mocking, but his moodiness passed, and he smiled at her.

"I think we'd better be getting back," she told him with some reluctance. The brief reprieve had been welcome, but she had a job to do.

"You're just as relentless as the tide." He sighed. "Work, work, work," he jeered gently.

"Would you rather we skipped this afternoon?" She searched his face for signs of overtiredness.

"I'm fine. Don't start up like Katie again."

"I like her. She seems nice."

"She likes you, too. So does Mitch." From his tone she guessed this was high praise.

"I don't think so," she disagreed. "Mitch seems to watch me so whenever he visits."

"I know. He says he can't sort you out. I told him I

couldn't either." Shane slowed his steps, forcing Jaclyn to stop and look up into his gray eyes. "What *is* it you're so vulnerable about, Jaclyn? Why do I keep feeling that you're hiding something from me?"

"Maybe I'm just as protective about my privacy as you are yours," she said lightly. "Shall we go in?"

He looked up and saw that they were standing before his house. "Sure." He sighed. "But I'll figure you out one day, Jaclyn."

No, you won't, Shane, you'll never understand, she thought to herself. You don't look as if anything has ever hurt you, not really deep down. You'd never, never understand. No one ever has.

They got back to the interview once inside, but Shane seemed quiet, introspective, hard to draw out. She asked him about his parents.

He looked at her. "I never told you about them, did I? My mother got me interested in this profession," he reminisced. "She often played extras. We lived near a movie lot, where I grew up, in California. It was a lot of fun, listening to her tell what had happened on the set that day. I remember how the three of us—she, Dad, and I—used to go to the theater and try to find her in the film when it appeared. She still does it sometimes now, to keep active, now that Dad's gone. She says there's a lot of call for 'older women,' as she considers herself. But she's as young as us, really, in her heart. Your father is dead, too, isn't he?" He turned the tables on her.

"How did you know?" She looked up from her notes, her expression guarded.

"I've heard you mention your mother, how you call her every few days. You told Katie she was a widow."

"So the two of you have been talking about me."

"Of course," he said grinning. "How else would I know that she liked you, as I said she did earlier? How is your mother, by the way?"

Jaclyn frowned. "I don't know. She sounded a little mysterious when I talked to her last night."

"Just like her daughter."

She shook her head. "I think something's going on, but I can't tell for sure. Last night she asked if I couldn't come home a little sooner."

"You told her no?" he asked, his tone sharp.

Jaclyn nodded.

"You haven't told me about your father."

She frowned more deeply. "He died a few years back." She flipped through the list of questions she'd written down the night before. "There was something else I wanted to ask, before I forget."

"You don't want to talk about it, eh?"

She looked up. "No," she said bluntly. "Now, have you any plans for marriage?" It was a question sure to get him off the subject at hand.

"Are you offering?" he shot back, amused.

She flushed. "Of course not."

"What a pity."

"Well?"

"Yes," he told her.

"Soon?" Why did his answer give her such a curiously empty feeling? she asked herself.

He shrugged. "I'm not sure. I think so."

"What's her name?"

A grin spread across his face. "I'm not telling. You'll have to guess."

She chewed on her pencil, and spluttered when she found she'd put the lead end in her mouth by mistake. "Do I know her?"

"I don't know how to answer that. Yes, I guess you do." His words were cryptic, his expression unfathomable.

"What does that mean? Either I know her or I don't." She was becoming slightly exasperated.

"It's not always that simple."

"It should be. But you won't be honest with me, will you? You have to sit there and play games with me, parrying words back and forth, arguing over their meanings." She leaned over to switch off her tape recorder. "Now you sound like Humpty Dumpty."

"How?"

" 'When *I* use a word, it means just what I choose it to mean—neither more nor less.' "

He laughed. "Okay, I take the hint. But I never promised to be cooperative, did I?"

"Would you have kept that promise, in any case?" she asked tartly.

"No. Probably not, little cat. Teasing you is just too much fun. Where are you going?" he asked as she stood up.

"I'm going back to the hotel," she told him, scooping her notes and tape recorder into her carryall. She picked up her purse and slung it onto one shoulder. "I think we've both had enough for today. You look tired." But deep inside her, she knew that it was Shane's unexpected answer to her question about his marriage plans that had disconcerted her, worried her. But why?

"I'm not," he was saying. "Stay, and I'll try to be more cooperative."

Jaclyn shook her head and smiled sweetly. "I don't think you can be."

"Why, you little—" He was on his feet, but she was already out the door and running lightly down the dunes.

The elusive sound of her laugh drifted up on the breeze from the sea.

CHAPTER SEVEN

"That's the first time you've asked me about racing. Why?" Shane wanted to know.

Jaclyn looked up from her notepad. "No particular reason. I *do* keep my questions about one subject separate from another. Hadn't you noticed that?" But it really was because she couldn't avoid them any longer. Shane must not find out why she hadn't asked them before.

"Oh, yes." He gave an exaggerated, weary-sounding sigh and leaned back into the cushions of the sofa. "I remember once we argued a whole morning about my being a supposed director on the set."

"I didn't—" she began hotly, breaking off when she saw that he was grinning.

"I'm teasing! What's the matter with you this morning? You look a little tired."

She shrugged. "I didn't sleep well, that's all."

"Is something bothering you?" he asked, his gray eyes intent on her face. His hand trailed lightly up her arm.

"No, of course not. I think I'll need a vacation to rest up from this one, that's all." She edged away from his hand, but there wasn't much space to get away from him on the smaller sofa he'd persuaded her to sit upon beside him, and it was even harder to avoid that unnerving stare of his, she thought nervously.

"Then why don't we knock off for a day?"

"No!" she said a trifle more sharply than she intended. "I mean, I'd just as soon get it over with today. I think this will probably be the last session I'll be needing with you." She was going to have to find a way to tell him that she was leaving at the end of the week.

"No more needling me with questions?" he jibed. But he didn't look as happy as she'd thought he would. He got up and restlessly prowled the room, finally stopping before the fireplace to lean an elbow on the mantel and stare moodily at the trophies that rested on it.

Jaclyn waited, pencil poised above her notepad. The tape ran silently in the recorder. As minutes passed she found her thoughts drifting. After tomorrow she'd no longer need to walk down the beach to his house to sit and question and talk and argue. To go for walks with him— She jerked to attention when his hand touched her cheek. "What?"

"You were a million miles away," he told her, and she found the nearness of his face, his mouth to hers even more unnerving than his previous closeness had been. "What were you daydreaming about?"

"I was giving you time to decide if you wanted to talk— about the racing, I mean," she lied.

He stared at her incredulously. "And you were going to leave it at that?"

"Uh, well . . ." she faltered.

"You'd probe so deeply into everything else and not ask about that?"

"Well, I don't know. I thought you might be supersti-

147

tious about the subject after, after . . ." She hesitated to use the word.

"After my crash?" he inserted brusquely. He rubbed the scar near his hairline in an unconscious gesture as he turned to stare again at the trophies. "I never have been. Then it happened, the very day I was about to announce— Go ahead, ask your questions."

"Announce what?"

"Never mind. Go on with them."

Jaclyn wanted to argue with him, keep at him until he told her what he'd started to say. But she'd tried that before, and it had never worked with Shane. He always remained adamant in his refusal to answer a question, or managed to find a way to distract her somehow. She'd like to forget about questions that would upset either of them today, but she couldn't. There would be no other day.

"You know, I'd understand if you didn't want to talk about the racing," she ventured to say.

"You would?" He smiled at her mockingly. "What do you understand?"

"I've heard about drivers being superstitious," she repeated.

"What have you heard?" He came to sit beside her again, so close that their thighs touched, and the scent of his after-shave drifted over to her as he put his arm along the back of the sofa. His hand played with a lock of her hair, disconcerting her.

"Some—sometimes they don't like to talk about the future," she stammered. "I guess that's a superstition I can understand better than some of the other things that bother them."

"Such as?" His hand tucked her hair behind one ear,

and with one long finger he traced the convolutions of her earlobe, not taking much interest in the conversation.

"Oh, their not wanting to drive a car painted the color green, or bearing the number thirteen. And—" She stopped, realizing she was saying too much, when an alert expression came over his face, and the delicious motions of his touch on her ear stopped abruptly. He prompted her to go on, but she shook her head. "It's not that important."

"You sound as if you know quite a bit about it. Where did you get that knowledge?"

She searched in her mind for an excuse. "Gino is rather superstitious. I've probably picked up a lot of it from him."

"I wouldn't have thought you and Gino did much talking," Shane remarked with a trace of sarcasm.

She stiffened. "What are you implying?"

"Let's just say that I noticed how possessive he was of you. And I saw the two of you in that tight clinch at Mitch's party, remember?"

Blushing, she told him it was none of his business. "Let's get back to *our* business."

"Why did Gino leave a beautiful woman like you behind, anyway? Especially when he knew you'd be seeing me?" Shane went on, ignoring her last remark.

"I told you before, Gino is like a brother to me, nothing more."

"Funny. That wasn't the impression he gave me when he visited me at the hospital. Don't look so surprised. He felt the need to warn me off, apparently. How did you meet Gino, anyway?"

"My family visited Italy once, and that's where we met

the Spinnellis," she said lightly. "Now, if you don't mind, I've got quite a lot of questions for you today."

"You're doing it again. You just can't have me asking a personal question, can you?"

"When and why did you start racing?" she asked, ignoring his last words.

There was silence. She looked up from her notes to find him watching her, black eyebrows drawn in a frown. Their eyes met, clashed in a battle of wills, and then he sighed.

"Okay, okay, business first." He gave in with obvious reluctance. "Let's see. It was when I had to do some research for a role. They let me sit in a race car, then take it for a spin, a slow one, around the track. That was it. I was bitten by the racing bug, or whatever you call it."

"Lured by the metal mistress," she muttered to herself.

"What?"

"Nothing. Go on."

"Well, after that it didn't matter what sort of car I raced, or what race or prize I might win. It was a new challenge, a way to test myself. I try to be the best I can possibly be at everything I attempt, and this is such a precise and demanding sport that it has a terrific appeal for me."

"Is it still a challenge?"

"Not as much as one I've discovered lately." He moved even closer, and she didn't need to ask what—or rather, who—he referred to.

"You say you have no favorite race, yet you consistently enter the twenty-four-hour race here. Why?"

He raised an eyebrow. "Your research again, eh?"

"There wasn't really very much in those files. You remind me of Garbo, the way you avoid the press."

"If I'd known what a pleasure it is to have someone like

you interview me, I'd have done it long ago. I told you that before, remember?"

"Are you being sarcastic?"

"You don't find this enjoyable?" he cross-questioned.

She sighed. "We still seem to fight over my questions and your answers. Or shall I say you avoid them when you don't just give me half-answers."

"Now, I thought I was being cooperative today."

"Then why are we off the track again?" she retorted tartly.

Shane sent his eyes heavenward. "Forgive me. Let's get on with the inquisition, please. You were asking why I raced here more often than other places. It's because I love the area and the racecourse."

"Why do you like it here?"

"Which, the course or the area?"

"The course. You already told me why you love the area. At the Spinnelli party, remember?"

"I remember everything about that night." His voice was soft, sensuous.

Jaclyn flushed. "If you're referring to Gino's disgusting conduct—"

"I wasn't," he soothed. "I was thinking about how enjoyable it was. Yes, enjoyable," he said, and it was her turn to look incredulous.

"All we did was fight!"

"Not us. Well, not at first, remember? Ah, I see you remember."

"But that's all past," she told him, trying to brush aside the mood of intimacy their shared memories evoked. "Just because we're fighting less these days, it shouldn't give you the impression we're friends or—"

"Jaclyn," he interrupted her, "it's not something our

151

fighting or not fighting will change. We've both known we were attracted to each other from the start."

It was true; she had to admit it to herself. They'd been getting along beautifully until Gino had intruded. "But after you learned I was a journalist, everything changed," she pointed out. "It can't ever be the same, can it?"

He let out an exasperated sigh. "I told you that I've changed my opinion of you and your profession. Especially after knowing how hard you work; how you care about getting the truth about someone."

"Which I'm not getting right now."

"Okay, okay. Where were we? Oh, yes, the course. I really enjoy the challenge of an endurance race such as this one. It puts the driver and the car on trial as no other. This isn't a race of just speed or skill. It's also a test of whether you can stick in there for the full twenty-four hours, through day and night and any weather conditions or problems with the car. And the course is one of the best for this type of race. There's the safety of a race conducted under the supervised conditions of a racecourse, with the crowd getting to watch all of the action."

Jaclyn leaned forward to change tape cassettes as Shane told her Mitch could take most of the credit for his racing at Daytona. "He talked me into racing here, and I haven't been sorry. He also introduced me to my co-driver. I think he had hopes of talking me into racing internationally."

"Why *don't* you do the international circuit?"

"Because I've never had the time in between film commitments. You know, you make it sound as if racing is my principal interest."

She looked at him levelly. "Isn't it?"

Shane laughed. "Of course not. I'm an actor, remember? I was before I raced, and I will be after I finish racing."

"You'd give up racing?" she asked, not hiding her disbelief.

"Yes, of course. This race is one of the very few I enter these days. As a matter of fact, after the last race, I was going to—" He broke off, and a guarded look came across his face. "Racing is just *one* of my interests."

"But it's such an all-consuming one, isn't it?"

"You know, if this is something else you've learned from Gino, then maybe I'll change my mind about him. Yes, for some, it *is* an all-consuming passion. But not for others; not in the same ways, either. Remember that I'm not like Gino, for instance. He is and probably always will be a race driver, or will be connected somehow with the sport. For him, there's nothing else he's ever wanted to do. But some men go on to other careers, do other things—"

"Or die before they get a chance to," she said flatly. It was out before she knew what she was saying.

"There was almost a touch of bitterness in your voice. Why?"

She feigned surprise. "Was there?" she asked with all the innocence she could muster. "I was just stating a fact. Racing is a dangerous sport. You can't deny that."

"I never said it wasn't," he said with a touch of impatience. "But so's crossing the street, and you wouldn't want to stay on one side of it all your life, would you? Who wants to be safe and never *live,* never take a chance for fear you'll be hurt or fall on your face? Maybe that's why you fight what's happening between us. No, don't pretend you don't know what I'm talking about. You can't always protect yourself from getting hurt, Jaclyn. You have to stop being afraid to feel. Stop hiding in your shell. Come out and trust me. Jaclyn?"

She looked away from the seductive appeal in his eyes. "Can—can we get back to *my* questions, *please?*"

Shane rubbed his hands over his face, peering out at her for a moment between his parted fingers. Then he sighed and nodded.

"Has the accident changed your mind about racing?"

"No. Why would it?"

"You'll try again?" Jaclyn found herself holding her breath.

"Why wouldn't I?"

She expelled her breath silently. "Will you race again?"

His features became stony. "What the hell are you implying?" he snarled. "That I've turned chicken since the accident? That I'm afraid to race because of it?"

"No, that's the last thing in the world I'd think! Please, I didn't mean that!"

He ran his hands through his thick black hair. "I'm sorry, I should have known better. You had to ask that question. I'm sure a lot of people are wondering. They'll think that, won't they, if I don't go back and enter another race?" He looked thoughtful.

"No, no, Shane, they won't! People would understand if you didn't want to—"

"Who said I didn't?" he interrupted, watching her closely. "Did you think I might not?"

"It doesn't matter what I think."

"Yes, it does. To me." He moved closer, lifting her chin with his hand, forcing her to stare into his eyes. "What would *you* have me do, Jaclyn?" His voice was softly caressing, gently urging, so that she almost told him, *"Don't, please, I couldn't bear to see you hurt again!"*

His hand slid back to cup the nape of her neck as his mouth covered hers in a kiss that shook her senses. "You don't have to answer me, Jaclyn," he said huskily. "Your eyes do. Why don't you want me to?"

"It—it's so dangerous, Shane. The next time you could —" She broke off, pulling from his arms. She jumped to her feet, crossing the room to stand and stare out the window at the sea. She couldn't let him see the fear that lurked in her eyes. But he was behind her, pulling her around relentlessly to face him.

"What if I said that it's going to be my last race, Jaclyn?" he asked quietly.

"Oh, come on! That's just an excuse!" she cried. "That's what so many drivers say when they know they should quit, when they feel their luck might soon run out. But racing's like a drug in the system—after a while the addict needs that very thing that can kill him to live," she said a little wildly. She tried to pull away from him, but he wouldn't let her.

"Jaclyn, where did you get a crazy idea like that?" He stared at her, incredulous.

The fight went out of her. "What does it matter?" she asked dully, shaking her head.

"Could it be that you care a little?" His voice was gentle.

Emotions raged within her, out of control like a brakeless car. She couldn't deny it. But she couldn't love him. She wouldn't! It would destroy all her hard-won serenity. She'd never find any peace with this disturbing man, and when he offered her a life that was so like one she had known, that had caused her such pain— Wait a minute! She caught her runaway thoughts. He hasn't offered anything at all! "No, it's impossible!" She fought his hands, but he wouldn't let her free.

"Jaclyn, what's the matter with you? For God's sake, what have I said that's so terrible? Would it be so awful to admit that you care about me?"

"Yes!"

His eyes narrowed. "Why do you keep fighting your feelings about me? I know how you feel— No, don't shake your head at me—I do!" His mouth descended on hers again, robbing her of speech, or the inclination to resist him. He explored her lips and the moistness within, then her cheeks, the curving line of her throat, while his hands explored her body with all the erotic effort to learning the physical taste and feel of her that she'd been devoting to learning about him emotionally.

Bells rang, and Jaclyn came to realize it was the doorbell. "Shane, somebody's at the door. *Shane.*"

With a backward, almost anguished look at her, he finally tore himself from her and strode to the door.

"I'm so sorry, Shane, I forgot my key, and you didn't hear me knocking at the back door." It was Katie. She glanced apologetically at Jaclyn, who was surreptitiously trying to restore order to her appearance, then back at Shane. Mumbling "Hope I haven't interrupted anything," she hurried toward the kitchen.

"Maybe it's as well that she did," Shane said, running his hands through his hair in a distracted gesture.

Jaclyn turned from his probing look and stared out at the ocean, tensing a little when she felt him slide his hands over her shoulders. She hadn't heard his steps on the rug.

"So tense." His voice was a low, caressing whisper near her ear as his hands, warm and supple, kneaded the muscles of her shoulders. But the motion of his massage was sensuous, anything but comforting, and when he pushed the hair from the back of her neck and his mouth touched the nape, Jaclyn jumped away from him. She moved back to the sofa, bending to pick up her notepad, but he was right beside her, plucking it from her fingers.

"What are you doing?"

"Closing up shop." He held out a hand to her. "I think we've both had enough for a while. Let's go down to the beach, to see if it doesn't relax you."

"I'm fine," she said quickly. But she wasn't really. And she knew what a tempting invitation it was to go for a walk, all the more so because she wouldn't be staying much longer. He didn't know that yet. Now she wanted to get the racing questions over and done with. *Today.* "I don't know." She looked at him doubtfully. "I'm so close to being finished."

"Let's explore it all down on the beach," he urged. "And who knows. Maybe I can get behind this screen of mystery you've got in front of you."

That decided her. "No. If you're going to use it as an opportunity to probe at me, then forget it. I'd rather stay here and get on with business."

He sighed. "I'll answer your questions on the beach, then, okay?"

But when they were seated on a beach blanket minutes later, she found that he had no intention of being cooperative as he'd promised. "No comment," he replied to one, two, then three questions.

"You lied to me!" she accused.

"So I did," he said, stretching out on his side and facing her. "But I think you've lied to me a couple of times, haven't you? The few times I was able to get the least little bit of information about you."

"No one else I've interviewed has wanted to know about me," she told him, sidestepping his casual accusation.

"Is that still the only way you see me? As the person you're interviewing?" He sounded exasperated.

"Of course," she told him—no, lied to him! "How else should I?"

"This way." His head blotted out the sun, and his mouth was on hers again, fiercely demanding a response from her. It wasn't just his expertise that drew what he wanted from her, and they both knew it when he lifted his head to stare at her, his eyes burning with a banked fire.

She pushed at him and sat up, combing her fingers through her hair and not looking at him. "Why did you do that?" she demanded, but her voice was shaky and her lips had difficulty forming the words.

"Look at me, Jaclyn." His voice was soft, compelling.

She stared stubbornly at the sea, so that all he could see was her profile, half-hidden by the dark-gold hair that blew gently in the breeze.

"I told you there was something," he insisted with almost arrogant pleasure.

"So what, Shane? What have you proved?" she burst out, stung by the knowledge that he'd felt her response.

"Shh, be quiet," he warned. "We don't want to spoil things." He gestured at the people around them, and she remembered what he'd said about the anonymity that wasn't an eccentricity, but a necessity for him to lead a normal life.

She dug her fingers into the sand and let it drift through them.

"Why the sigh?"

She looked up. "I guess I never really appreciated privacy. You just don't have the freedom to come and go as I thought."

He shrugged. "Let's not talk about it now. Listen, would you like to drive back to the hotel for a swimsuit?"

"I thought you weren't allowed to drive yet?" she asked suspiciously.

"Darn that woman!" he muttered.

"Besides, isn't it a little cool in the water yet?"

He shrugged. "Usually it's the visitors who think the water's fine when the locals think it's chilly. Well, if you won't, I will." He stood and stripped off his shirt. It revealed a chest broad and muscular, tanned a rich bronze.

Jaclyn remembered the feel of crisp dark hairs, the warmth of his skin against her hand that day he'd forced his kiss on her, on the beach near her hotel. She glanced away in embarrassment as she felt Shane's eyes on her.

"Something bothering you?" he asked, sounding amused.

"Of course not." She drew her knees up to her chest and sat, her chin on her arms, folded across them, studiously avoiding looking at the virile body standing so near her. Obviously Shane had intended coming down on the beach today, for he now had pulled off his slacks and stood before her dressed in swimming briefs. "I'm only thinking that it's a surprise you didn't figure out a way to have *me* bring a swimsuit, since you seem to have planned this today," she told him, indicating his swimming attire.

"Tomorrow you'll be sure to bring it, won't you?" He grinned.

"Don't be so sure," she snapped.

He ran down the beach to plunge into the surf and swim out to sea. He appeared to have no fear. She watched him stroke far out into the water. Lifeguards weren't on duty this time of the year. Their big red chairs lay on their sides high up on the sand, looking like giant highchairs tossed askew. But someone like Shane scoffed at danger, anyway, she reflected. He'd probably not swim here if there was someone looking over his safety.

Shane bodysurfed in, his golden skin gleaming as he went in and out of foam-capped waves. Drops of water glistened in dripping rivulets that ran down his body.

"Hey, don't!" she cried indignantly when he stood near her and shook the drops from him like a dog, showering her.

He laughed and dropped to the beach blanket, wiping his body with his shirt before putting it back on.

"How was the water?"

He snatched her hand and slid it under his shirt. "Must have been warm enough for me. I'm not cold, am I?"

She jerked her hand from him. "Stop that!"

They sat for a while and watched the antics of a little boy with hair the color of newly minted pennies playing further down the beach. He attempted to throw a Frisbee to his older brother, who ran to fetch it and threw it back. Jaclyn had to smile at the sight of the youngster who had to stop now and then to clutch at a diaper, dragged down by seawater—or other wetness!—making it cling perilously to his hips. The sport between the two caught the attention of two young girls who were walking past. They evidently decided that talking to the little brother about his prowess with the spinning disc could lead to an introduction to the good-looking older one.

"That young man has found that his little brother and the Frisbee attract more girls than anything else he's tried," Shane told her with a chuckle.

"So you've watched him and his girl-gathering tricks, have you?"

"Of course. You never know when you can learn something new," he said with a grin.

"I'll bet you know all the tricks," she muttered to herself.

"What did you say?"

"Nothing. Is that all you watch when you come down here?"

He shook his head and told her about what a romantic place the beach was. Not just for the young people, he said, but for older people, too, retired couples who now could call their time their own and spend it together. She listened to him with rapt fascination, seeing and hearing a sensitive side of him that he didn't often show.

And when a car engine whirred to life but the car couldn't move, caught in sand not far from them, she saw another side of Shane, too, an unpretentious, fun-loving Shane, who took her hand and ran with her down to help get it unstuck. He showed her how to cup her hands and dig the sand from behind the tires. When the car was free the driver, the mother of a carful of boisterous children, thanked them and drove off. A small blue plastic shovel came flying from the car window, to land at Jaclyn's feet. Failing to get the mother's attention, Shane turned and presented it to Jaclyn.

She laughed and accepted it as they walked back to their spot near Shane's house. "That was hard work," she told him, dropping down on the blanket. "But it was fun. Does that happen often?"

Collapsing on the blanket beside her, Shane told her how it wasn't only the visitors who parked too high on the softer sand, but sometimes local people as well. She laughed at his story of a car caught one day in the tide, when the driver had done the opposite and parked too close to the incoming tide. The driver of a van had stopped to offer assistance, and had tied a rope to the car to tow it. But he'd only succeeded in getting his vehicle stuck as well. Finally a wrecker had arrived to pull them both out, and Shane said the whole thing made him think of a circus parade of elephants with their trunks around the tail of the animal before them. When he recalled another story, of a policeman who'd stopped to warn a driver and had parked too close to the water, then turned to find the tide had crept up around his patrol car, Jaclyn couldn't stop laughing. Shane's word picture was so vivid, Jaclyn could see the poor officer of the law—seawater creeping up his crisply uniformed legs, an embarrassed flush working its way up to his hat, until the wrecker arrived—as if it were happening right then before her.

"I haven't ever seen you laugh like that." There was a curious expression in Shane's eyes. "You look so different when you aren't serious."

"You act like I go around poker-faced," she said lightly, conscious that his mood was changing, becoming more serious than she wanted.

"No, far from it," he admitted. "But I like it when you smile and laugh like that." He reached out to caress her cheek with his hand.

Something electric passed between them, a moment of supercharged stillness in which she could hear her heart pounding within her chest. Her breath caught in her throat as she stared into his eyes, mesmeric in their intensity. "I—I'm sure that you must have met many beautiful women in Hollywood."

"Maybe. But you intrigue me. It's not just that you're

beautiful. You have a sensitivity about you—with your words, your feelings, your actions. And there's an attractive, vulnerable side of yourself that you try to hide with coolness. Jaclyn, come on, tell me about yourself,'' he urged quietly. "Tell me what it is you hide from others. From me. I promise you I won't take advantage of it, whatever it is. I wouldn't hurt you. You *have* been hurt, haven't you?"

She stared at him in amazement. That faultless intuition of his—how he could seem to read her very thoughts! Here, in this peaceful setting, the ocean moving in and out with liquid music, the sunshine golden and warm on their shoulders, it would be so easy to loosen up, to confide. But still she hesitated, biting her lower lip between her teeth.

"What's hurt you, Jaclyn?" he pressed her. "A man?"

"Not exactly. It wasn't an affair or anything like that."

"I thought not. You have an untouched quality about you." Then, when she shifted uncomfortably he added, "Don't retreat from me again, Jaclyn. Go on. Tell me where you live," he said, changing the subject a little. "You told me you lived with your mother in New York. Tell me what you like about the city."

It seemed a safe enough subject, so Jaclyn told him how she loved the hustle and bustle of people moving about the city, its diversity, yet how she hated its impersonality and the noise. Watching the soaring and gliding of a sea gull doing an air dance in the sky above her, lulled by the mood of the beach, and the easy way Shane drew her out, she found herself confessing that she loved all the freedom and space he had there, envied him for it. . . .

"You really like it here, don't you?" There was warmth and understanding in his voice.

"I love it," she acknowledged with a smile. "I'd love to

163

live here by the sea and write the novel I've always wanted to—" She stopped and blushed, feeling she'd said too much. She'd never told anyone, not even her mother, about the novel.

"There, you did it again. You were coming out of your shell, but now you're trying to go back inside it," he chided her. "Have you ever let *anyone* get close to you, Jaclyn?"

"Not really," she had to admit.

"Do it with me," he urged. "Let me get close to you, Jaclyn."

"No!" She threw up her hands in a protective gesture, but he hadn't moved closer. "I—I can't. And I don't want to. I don't want a star ride for a few weeks, until you tire of me, Shane."

"What?" His voice was explosive with anger, and his hands gripped her shoulders. "Tell me what that crack was supposed to mean," he demanded.

"I won't be just a dalliance." Tears blurred her vision as the pain of his hands and his voice bit into her. "I want a different relationship with a man than that."

"What makes you think— I could prove that's not— Oh, hell, this isn't the time. Or the place." He pulled off his sunglasses and rubbed at his eyes in a tired, defeated motion. "Damn, I've got to get out of the sun, it's giving me a headache. Let's go back to the house so I can take something for it."

Was it the sun, or the argument they'd been having? she wondered guiltily, knowing he still suffered headaches from the concussion. "No, Shane, I think I'll go back to the hotel."

"But you'll come back later? We'll have dinner together."

"Will Katie be there?" she asked casually, shaking sand from the blanket.

"No. I suppose that means you won't come." It was a statement, not a question, and before she could nod he said, "Let's go out, then."

"But I thought you couldn't—"

"There's a place here where no one will bother us. Will you come? Please, Jaclyn?" he coaxed.

She was puzzled by his mood, disturbed by the way he was trying so hard to persuade her, yet she wanted to be with him.

"All right," she gave in, promising to be ready in an hour. I'll tell him tonight that I'm leaving soon, she decided as she walked down the beach to the hotel.

When the low-slung, wine-colored car drew up at the hotel entrance an hour later, Jaclyn walked out quickly. A doorman hurried to open her door, a little curious about the driver's identity. That's what the notoriety in the paper had done, she thought with a wry smile. That, and the knowledge that Jaclyn was supposed to be interviewing Shane somewhere in the city. She was aware that the hotel staff watched her comings and goings with interest, but no one had asked her any questions about him.

"What's the smile for?" he wanted to know as they drove off.

She told him about the staff's curiosity, and he asked if it bothered her. He seemed pleased when she said it didn't. He looked lost in thought, and they didn't talk much during the short drive. Like Gino, he proved to be a careful and considerate driver on the city streets. But Jaclyn wasn't surprised. Most race drivers were. Either they got their speed urge out at the racetrack, or they just knew better than to drive fast in traffic. Shane wore his seat belt, and he'd waited until Jaclyn had buckled up before driving away.

He helped her out of the car at the door of an elegant little restaurant overlooking the ocean. Inside, an obsequious maître d' led them to a candlelit table tucked out of sight from the other diners. From the service Shane was given and the way she noticed he ordered without a menu, Jaclyn guessed that he had been a frequent patron while in town. Their drinks were brought, and then they were left alone.

The inside of the restaurant was decorated to resemble a pirate's secret cave, with all the trappings of a sea-going pirate, lit only by dozens of candles scattered about. It gave diners the impression that they had stumbled on the place where at any moment a swarthy privateer might swagger in to sit and covet his stolen treasures—and might bring a woman and look at her the way Shane was looking at Jaclyn then, as if he wanted to covet the woman, too, like the precious things he hoarded. Why had Shane brought her here? she wondered to herself.

"You wore it."

Jaclyn glanced down at her dress. He'd asked her to wear it. "I didn't have much else packed. I was surprised that you remembered it. I mean, I wore it that night when you—" She broke off, blushing.

"When I stormed into Mitch's party and raised hell about that newspaper picture," he said without a trace of rancor. "You looked beautiful in it. But even more beautiful tonight. Candlelight seems to give you a golden glow. But then I know that you're not the cool blonde you try to pretend to be." His hand reached across the table to touch her fingers, which were fingering the stem of her water glass nervously.

166

"The band's here tonight," he said as the sensuous sounds of music drifted across the room. "Let's dance," he urged.

He drew her into his arms on the dance floor, and when the warmth and closeness of his body was against her, Jaclyn knew again what a devastating effect he had on her senses. For the night, the Shane who bantered and teased and argued and aggravated her beyond measure was gone, replaced by this perfect lover. And yet whatever his mood, Shane could disturb her. Even when they argued she felt an exhilaration, an aliveness, she hadn't ever felt before with a man.

Jaclyn closed her eyes as they danced slowly around the dance floor. His hand pressed her closely to him as they danced. Others moved around them, but she was in a dream in which they were alone with the blissful music and the sounds of the nearby sea.

The music stopped, and they reluctantly moved back to their table. For her, Shane had ordered Florida rock lobster served in the shell. It was delicious, but Jaclyn toyed with her food and sipped nervously at her wine.

"Shane? Why . . . are you acting so different tonight?"

He smiled, the gleam of his white teeth startling against the rich bronze tan he'd regained since the accident. "I'm only the way I've wanted to be since I've known you. But you wouldn't let me get closer," he said softly. "By the way, I have something for you." He reached into the inside pocket of his suit and withdrew a small velvet-covered box. "Jaclyn, what's the matter?" he asked in concern. "You've gone white!"

"N-nothing," she said nervously. "I'd—I'd rather you didn't give me anything, Shane."

He raised a dark eyebrow and watched her with an

unreadable expression. "It's not what you think, Jaclyn," he said.

Her cheeks flamed. "You don't know what I'm thinking."

"Oh, yes, I do. Open it." He pushed the box toward her.

She opened it with fingers that shook a little. It was a perfect little golden sand dollar, patterned after the real ones she'd searched for each day on the beach to take home with her.

"It's for your charm bracelet," he told her when she raised her eyes and thanked him.

To take home. She hadn't yet told him that she'd made plane reservations and called her mother to let her know when she was arriving. Perhaps now was the time.

"Excuse me?" She'd been trying so hard to find the words to tell him that she hadn't heard him.

"Why aren't you wearing the bracelet?"

"No special reason. I'll have this put on right away. Thank you again, Shane. I'll treasure it when I've gone back home."

"I wanted to talk to you about that. I don't want you to go back, Jaclyn, at least—"

"It *is* him!" a strident female voice interrupted. "Oh, look, Tom, I told you it was Shane Jaeger. I *knew* I recognized him on the dance floor. Mr. Jaeger, sign an autograph for me. I just *have* to show it to my bridge club." She shoved paper and pencil at him.

"Excuse me, madam, but I'd rather not be disturbed right now," Shane said as politely as he could, but Jaclyn could tell he was irritated.

The woman bristled. "Well, you're too good to give your fans a few minutes of your time! Maybe if you don't, one day you might not be asked, Mr. High-and-Mighty. Why, when I—"

"Is there some problem, Mr. Jaeger?" It was the maître d'. "May I be of some assistance?"

The woman's escort was trying to lead the indignant woman away, obviously embarrassed by her stream of invective against the now coldly angry Shane.

"If you'd just see that we're left alone . . ." Shane said in a low voice. "Tell the woman to leave her name and address with you, and I'll send her an autograph, *anything.* Just get them out of here." His jaw was rigid with suppressed anger.

The man did his best, but by now all eyes in the restaurant were on their table. Jaclyn was mortified with embarrassment. She tried to raise her glass calmly to her lips, but it started slipping from her nerveless fingers, and made a *clink!* when it touched her plate. The sound of it nearly shattered her.

"Jaclyn, don't let that upset you," Shane soothed. "It happens sometimes, but it doesn't have to spoil our evening."

She raised her eyes, shimmering with unshed tears. "Please, can we go? I can't stand everyone staring at me like this, after that awful woman!"

"I don't know what to say, Jaclyn," he told her when they were finally in the car and driving away from the restaurant. "I had hoped for a much better evening. But it doesn't have to end now. Shall we go somewhere else? Or back to my place for coffee?"

She shook her head miserably. "No, please, Shane. I'd just like to go back to my hotel."

He drove the car down onto the beach, driving slowly beside the ocean, glinting silver beneath the moonlight.

Then, seeing her staring out her window, still upset, he uttered an oath under his breath. He parked the car and reached over for her. "Come on, now, Jaclyn, calm down." He drew her into his arms. "You get used to this sort of thing after a while," he soothed, his lips moving against her hair.

"Oh, Shane, if that's what you have to put up with, besides all the horrible things they print in the scandal magazines and everything. To think that I almost—" She broke off and burst into tears.

"What, Jaclyn? Come on, now, it's not worth crying about." He stroked her hair with a gentle hand.

It is, she thought miserably. And I could have made it worse for you! she thought. If I'd gone through with my original plans with that magazine, there would have been even more people like that awful woman in the restaurant bothering him. As it was, she felt terrible remembering how close she'd come to being that vindictive.

"Better now?" he asked as she finally lay quiet against him. When she nodded he lifted her face and kissed the tears from her cheeks. "Good. Let's go back to my place and talk. There's still something left unfinished." He started the car.

She knew her eyes were red-rimmed from crying, her hair was a mess, and her dress was crumpled from being held against him. But her appearance wasn't the only reason she didn't want to go there with him. Everything beautiful tonight now seemed just a dream, a dream that couldn't be. She knew that now more than ever, and if they went to his place, she wasn't sure she would be able to resist a passionate encounter like the one in the afternoon, when Katie had interrupted. She'd had enough emotional entanglements with Shane that day.

170

"No, please, take me to the hotel," she begged. "Please?"

He looked at her for a long moment and finally nodded. "I guess it's better if I do," he said. Was there regret in his deep voice? His eyes were dark and unreadable in the dimness of the interior of the car. "I guess we'll have to talk tomorrow. But I wanted to— Well, never mind." He shook his head.

But I wanted to— hung in the air as he drove her back to the hotel along the pale-sanded beach.

Wanted to what?

CHAPTER EIGHT

Jaclyn stirred her coffee and stared moodily out at the dismal day through the coffeeshop window overlooking the ocean. She shifted her gaze from the gray, churning sea to the coffee growing cold in the cup before her. Actually, it could have been a beautiful day and she would still have been depressed, still have been procrastinating, when she should be leaving to go to Shane's house, she admitted to herself. Pulling on the navy corduroy blazer that matched her slacks, she walked outside and stared up at the leaden sky. It was going to pour, and soon. There was a cool breeze blowing off the ocean, more the temperature she had expected to feel when she had stepped off the plane from New York, instead of the unexpected warmth of a Florida February.

She had to hurry, even though she didn't want to go to Shane's home, knowing things would be uncomfortable after the fiasco the night before.

It was disturbing that Shane hadn't been able to go out for a meal without having his privacy interrupted. If she had needed a reason not to be vindictive with the interview, she'd have had it last night. But it had been a long time since she had thought of revenge.

It had seemed, too, that Shane had changed in the way

172

he acted toward her. Last night hadn't been the first time they had dined together—she'd stayed for dinner at his house several times. But his mood had been different. Something about his seriousness had half-frightened her. She didn't know what he wanted from her, but he wasn't going to get it, she thought angrily, kicking at a clump of seaweed in her path. Her plane reservation had been moved forward. Back in New York City, she could try to forget this man who seemed to have the power to affect others so strongly, yet stay cool and unmoved about them.

"I will *not* love a man who doesn't love me! And, never, ever a man whose passion burns for the metal mistress!" she muttered aloud to herself as she walked along the water's edge. A rumble overhead alerted her to the imminent downpour. She quickened her steps, just as the sky seemed to open with a deluge of cool rain. Running the last few yards to Shane's house, she arrived a little breathless on the doorstep and rang the doorbell.

A clap of thunder sounded directly overhead, and as the sky was sliced by a jagged electric knife of brilliance, the door opened. A dark, almost satanic-looking figure stood in the doorway, startling Jaclyn.

"What is it?" Shane's voice echoed around her like the thunder. Then, as the sky was again streaked by lightning, he recognized her. "Jaclyn, what the hell are you doing here? Come inside out of the rain."

She stepped into the foyer, eager to be out of the storm, yet puzzled by Shane's behavior. Something was wrong, she sensed. Shane held a hand over his eyes in a gesture of pain as he stood before her, still dressed in a loosely belted bathrobe. He closed the door abruptly and turned and staggered, putting out a hand to the wall to steady himself.

"Shane, what is it?" she cried, concerned. She touched his arm, but he brushed her hand away.

"It's this damned head," he bit out.

Jaclyn strained her eyes to see in the dim light. His jaw was clenched, as if he were trying to fight the pain, conquer it with sheer willpower. "It came on during the night."

"Did you take the prescription the doctor gave you?" she asked anxiously as she followed his unsteady path into the living room. There, Shane slumped into a chair and massaged his temples in a tired, futile effort to relieve the pain. The dark circles under his eyes showed that he must have been up most of the night, suffering.

"Yes, but I've run out of it," he muttered. "I'll have to ride it out. I'd have had the prescription refilled, but I was hoping that I was over these migraines from the accident. After all, it's been nearly two weeks."

She shook her head in resignation. "Your head took a pretty hard blow, Shane, remember? It's no wonder you're still having headaches. I'm sorry you're in such pain."

"I don't need your blasted sympathy!" His voice was harsh.

She flinched at his words. "I—I'll go, then. I'm sorry I disturbed you. I wouldn't have come if I'd known." She turned quickly, so that he couldn't see the tears that had filled her eyes. But his hand shot out and grasped her wrist, stopping her.

"I'm sorry, Jaclyn," he apologized gruffly. "When Katie came I sent her home. I told her to call you and tell you to come later. I guess she didn't get you in time. Sometimes not having a telephone can be a damned nuisance. This head wouldn't let up enough for me to get to the one down the block to call you myself. I—" His face

174

whitened and he groaned. Closing his eyes, he rested his head on the back of his chair.

"Shane? I can go for your pills," she said hesitantly.

He opened his eyes, pain-dulled and leaden-gray in a face that bore the imprint of suffering. He stared at her for a moment, then closed them again and sighed.

"I guess I'll have to let you, won't I?" he muttered. "Take my car. The keys are in the kitchen on a hook near the door." He reached into the pocket of his robe, drew out a prescription bottle, and held it out to her.

"But the name on this bottle isn't yours!" she said in surprise. "It says Sam Jarrell on the label."

He managed a wry grin. "It couldn't very well say Shane Jaeger, could it? I made that mistake once, and people came to the door, bothering me."

"I'll be right back," she told him as she walked toward the kitchen.

"There's money in a jar on top of the refrigerator," he called to her.

She stared for a moment at the keys on the hook, then glanced over her shoulder. Shane couldn't see that she didn't take them. Why should she tell him she had no intention of driving his car? she asked herself as she left the house. He'd want to know why she didn't drive, probably demand that she stay at the house, when a short walk would bring the pills to relieve his pain. And she didn't care to explain herself about the car, anyway.

The storm had slackened to a drizzle. Her experience with Florida weather had shown her that rainy spells there were usually brief and mild. Besides, if the rain started again, she could always hail a taxi, she reasoned.

But on the way back the drizzle became a deluge, and she was thoroughly soaked when she let herself into the house. Shane's eyes widened as she handed him two of the capsules and a glass of water. Her hair hung in limp strands about her face, and her sodden clothes clung to her body in a way that made her blush when he looked her over.

"You got awfully wet," he muttered in a puzzled tone of voice. The effort of speaking was difficult now, with his pain so intense that she could almost feel it radiate out to her. She had never seen anyone suffer a migraine. It seemed unbelievable that Shane could endure that kind of pain and not fall unconscious.

Jaclyn shrugged, acting unconcerned about her condition. "Can I get you anything else?" She changed the subject.

He got up from the chair and stood before her, unsteady on his feet. "I'm going to lie down upstairs for a few minutes and let these capsules work. Go take off those wet things and throw them in the dryer. There's a robe on the back of the bathroom door."

"No, I'd better be going." She backed away. "I'll come back tomorrow," she said. Then she remembered that she was leaving soon, and still hadn't had the chance to tell him. And now wasn't the time.

"No!" he said sharply. "Please, I want to talk to you, and it won't wait until tomorrow. It's bad enough we were interrupted last night when—" He put his hands to his head. "Please, stay?" Something about his quiet, coaxing words compelled her to change her mind.

"All right," she agreed, not wanting to argue with him in his condition. She watched him climb the stairs to his bedroom.

Jaclyn found the robe and pulled it on after stripping off her wet clothes. It was soft and warm, a forest-green velour with sleeves she had to fold up to uncover her hands. The hem fell past her knees, and when she looked in the mirror she was totally surprised at her reflection.

It felt strange being in a male garment such as this, she thought. She looked different somehow. Vulnerable, perhaps. The scent of masculine soap clung to the robe. Her eyes were emerald-green in her pale face, wide and slightly apprehensive as she realized that she was in a man's robe for the first time, alone with him in his house. The thought disturbed her. She quickly bent and scooped up her wet things and went downstairs to put them into the dryer.

Shane had lit a fire in the fireplace while she was at the pharmacy. Jaclyn sat before it on the thick carpeting and dried her hair. Outside, the sea winds blew sheets of rain against the windows, and the day grew darker. She felt warm and secure, in a way, yet she knew she didn't belong there. She got up to prowl restlessly about the room, idly picking up an exquisite shell from the collection on a glass shelf, studying a painting, staring out at the storm-tossed ocean.

Her clothes weren't ready when she checked, the heavy corduroy taking a long time to dry, so she returned to the living room. She spied a shelf of books and walked over to browse through them. Shane had a varied collection, everything from the arts and politics to best sellers and books on sports such as skydiving. There were also the books from which his films had been made, and a whole shelf devoted to racing. In the middle was a large, cumbersome book that drew her attention. She pulled it down and went to sit on the sofa, tucking her feet up under her. It was a thick, closely printed encyclopedialike book of "racing greats." Although the room was warm, Jaclyn shivered. But curiosity got the better of her. She found herself flipping through page after page, finding familiar faces. Some were gone now. Many, oh, too many, her mind cried soundlessly, had died in this sport. A tear trickled down her cheek as she found the picture of a friend of her father's. The accompanying paragraph stated dispassionately that the man had left behind a young family.

There was the poignant story of a racer whose prowess on the superhighways of speed was almost eclipsed by his popularity with women. Involved in a crash and knowing he might die, he had taken a last drag on a cigarette and flippantly urged his comrades to take care of his girl friends, telling them to "let that blonde in Cincinnati know I won't be able to make it tonight."

And then her fingers turned the page, and the jubilant face of her father seemed to spring up from it. Wearing a broad grin, he sat atop one of his racers, proudly holding up a victory cup. Jaclyn's mother was pictured, too, smiling, looking proud of her handsome husband. The small, pigtailed girl who stared a little shyly at the camera from her place between her parents was Jaclyn.

She abruptly put the book facedown on the table before her. The cover swam before her tear-filled eyes, a helmeted and goggled driver in his pioneer car merging in a crazy collage with his modern-day counterpart. She squeezed her eyes shut to block out the picture, and willed her tears not to fall. Oh, she was tired, so tired, of all this torment, she thought. I should have stayed back in New York. Why did I come here, only to upset all my hard-won composure by meeting a man like Shane? She could never sit in the stands and watch someone she loved race again, not after seeing her father killed. And seeing Shane injured had had the same effect on her. She couldn't, she wouldn't, expose herself to that kind of pain again! she told herself fiercely.

Jaclyn found herself drowsing. She couldn't let Shane come down and discover her dressed this way, she told herself. She must get up and see if her clothes were dry.
. . .

The jet whine of racers roared through her brain as technicolor dreams played across her mind screen, and she was once again watching her father race. It was a dream that always started happily. She and her mother watched from the stands with the families of other drivers, filled with pride at the skill Richard Lansing always showed on the course. And then the dream would change so suddenly, and all her happiness would go up in a cloud of acrid black smoke. Even before the smoke cleared she knew that the rescue workers would not be able to save her father.

"No! No, please don't let him die!" she screamed again and again as people restrained her from dashing down to help pull him out of the smoldering wreckage.

It was all so real. She was living it again, trapped in a nightmare from which she couldn't wake. Then the dream changed. Another racer was coming into view, a cobalt blue one, exploding into a ball of flame before her eyes. And inside was another man she loved—Shane Jaeger. Her screams began again.

Strong hands grasped her, shaking her until she was awake. "Jaclyn, wake up, it's only a bad dream. It's all right," a voice soothed. It was Shane who held her, comforted her, as she finally woke from the nightmare, sobbing. He held her tightly, his hands stroking her hair as he whispered soothing words, rocking her as if she were a child. Gradually her sobs quieted. But her heart continued to pound as she lay against his chest, bared to the waist by a yellow silk shirt tucked into cream-colored corduroy slacks. Something metallic pressed against her wet cheek. It was Shane's St. Christopher medal, something Jaclyn knew many drivers wore, whatever their religious preference.

Shane's hands rubbed the soft velour of the robe she wore. His robe. She stayed within the encircling arms even as a little warning voice in her mind told her that his hands no longer soothed. Now they were stroking, caressing her body pressed against his.

Shane pushed aside the silky layer of her hair, found the vulnerable softness of the nape of her neck. His mouth explored it, sending fiery shivers down her spine, moving along the curving line of her cheek and across her lips. And then the sensual exploration stopped.

His hands tilted her head back. He stared into her eyes—glowing emeralds in her pale face—a frown of concern creasing his forehead. There was a dark, unfathomable look in his eyes.

Her lips parted in unconscious invitation. The storm outside was building in intensity, but she barely heard it, her heart beating out the sounds of the thunder, the wind just a whisper compared to the rapid inhale and exhale of her breath. Inside, a sensual storm was building in them both that blocked out everything else.

They were aware only of each other. Nothing that surrounded them mattered. It had been the same that first time they had seen each other that day at the speedway, when all the people, all the noises, had been blotted out.

He was no longer the harsh, pain-tormented man she had met at the door. Bathed and shaven, the clean male scent of his body mingled with a masculine cologne that smelled tangy, inviting, like the sea outside.

His eyes were no longer a dull, leaden, gray, nor pain-filled. Now they glowed the warm color of coals long burned. She had once picked one up, as a child, thinking it cold. Its cool color was deceiving, belying the flame that still burned within. It had seared her tender palm, just as his eyes were threatening to scorch her body, half-revealed as the robe fell open.

She should move, get up, stop this, but when she stared into his eyes she was half-drugged with his nearness, mesmerized by the feeling that she was powerless against his attraction, like a moth too close to a flame, fascinated by its spiraling, burning beauty that held danger to tender flesh.

With exquisite agony, she felt his hands tighten on her arms as he pulled her closer, almost impatiently, lowering his mouth to hers with a muffled groan, pressing her body into the sofa cushions with his. His kiss was sensuous, masterful, giving yet stirring passion. She was unable to move, except against his hands as they pushed aside the velvety protectiveness of the robe, and his hands and mouth now sought what she was unable to withhold from him. He caressed the silky warmth of her skin until she felt inflamed, consumed by the wildfire of desire.

Shane raised his head and searched her face for the answer to an unspoken question. The flames from the fireplace cast flickering patterns of light across his face as he waited tensely for her answer, which was given without words. Then he was lifting her, carrying her without effort up the stairs to his bedroom.

He placed her in the center of the bed, and when her fingers fumbled with the belt of the robe, he knelt before her and untied it, pushing it from her shoulders. Moonlight entering the room through a skylight above the bed cast an unearthly loveliness over her nakedness.

"You're beautiful," he said softly. He stroked the soft fullness of her breasts, tracing the curves of her body with his hands.

He stood to shed his clothes, not taking his eyes from her, dressed only in moonlight, as she waited for him in his bed. A tall, powerful body emerged, muscles rippling along his shoulders as he stripped off his shirt. Jaeger—jaguar, she thought, watching his sinewy, naked body striding toward her like a jungle cat. But when he slid in beside her and drew her into his arms, she felt a twinge of fear and knew that she shivered.

"Cold?" he asked against her lips, gently catching her lower one between his teeth, biting it gently.

"N-no." But she couldn't keep herself from tensing up as his mouth slid down her neck.

He stopped. "What's the matter?"

"I—" She searched for words and failed. She shook her head miserably, feeling her face grow hot with shame.

Shane caught her chin with one hand, raised it so that she had to look up into his eyes. "What is it? Gino?"

"What?"

"Maybe you don't care for me the way I hoped you would. Is the thought of Gino stopping you?" His voice was grim.

She frowned, surprised at both his tone of voice and his question. "No. Why on earth should you think that? I told you I didn't love Gino."

"You've never slept with him?"

She shook her head.

"Why not?"

She remembered that night he had taken her for that wild ride after her eighteenth birthday party. Funny, she had always thought of Gino as a big brother. But his

182

feelings and actions hadn't been brotherly. He'd apologized later, but she had always looked at him differently after that. Italian men often expected to marry virgins, and yet he'd been willing that night to—

"Jaclyn?" Shane prompted, and now she felt his body tensing against hers.

"He—frightened me once. He still does a little. I never thought of him in that way."

"If that's not it, then what's bothering you?" His body relaxed, and she felt his hands slide behind her neck and massage it gently, relieving her tension. "Come on, look at me and tell me. Did you change your mind, Jaclyn?" Then he added, "You know, I've the strangest feeling you've not done this much before," he said musingly.

She tried to pull from his arms, but he wouldn't let her. "I—no," she admitted finally. "I haven't."

He went still. "Not even with someone other than Gino?"

She averted her head, and her hair fell, so that her expression was obscured. "No."

He sat up. "My God, a virgin!" he said in disbelief.

"Don't!" she burst out. "Don't act as if I'm—I'm—" She couldn't finish. What had that one man called her? An anachronism in this day and age! "I thought it wouldn't matter with . . ." She trailed off, realizing that she had almost said "with the man I love."

"With you," she finished miserably. She swung her legs off the bed and started to get up, but his hand stopped her.

"Where are you going?"

"To get dressed," she said, not turning to look at him.

He sighed. "If that's what you want."

Jaclyn turned to look at him with anguished eyes. "Shane, I—"

"No," he interrupted her gently. "I'm not going to try to change your mind, much as I'd like to. I wouldn't have brought you up here if I'd known."

She turned from him quickly, but not before he saw her expression. "Jaclyn, it's not because I don't want you. Is that what you're thinking? Come here," he said, pulling her, resisting, back into his arms when she nodded. She lay against his chest, wetting it with her tears for the second time that day, while he stroked her hair gently with his hands. "Do you know what you're offering me? I don't want to take something like that from you unless— Jaclyn, you're making this hard for me."

Did he know how hard *he* was making it for *her*? she wondered bitterly. "You probably want someone more experienced," she mumbled against his chest.

"No! I want you, you crazy little fool! I just never expected this."

She looked up at him. " 'Not in this day and age' is the line, I believe." There was bitterness in her voice.

"Do you mean someone's tried to make you feel like you're—"

" 'An oddball,' 'an anachronism,' 'incredibly old-fashioned,' " Jaclyn rattled off from memory.

Shane shook his head, his expression one of disbelief. "You're not an anachronism," he said.

She smiled tentatively, seeing his smile gleam in the dim light.

He framed her face with his hands and kissed her gently. "I'll admit there aren't many like you around these days, perhaps, but don't ever be embarrassed about it, Jaclyn."

"Sometimes"—she hesitated, then plunged ahead—

"sometimes I feel like a Model T in a crowd of new models," she confessed.

"You're not any antique," he admonished. "If you must use that comparison, then you're a special edition, something rare and precious after an assembly line of cheap imitations, Jaclyn, and worthy of being cherished. And not because of your virginity, but because all of you is very special. Now I understand that air you have, that vulnerability you've built up around yourself."

"I . . . find it hard to open up around people sometimes, Shane. I can't help being shy." She was surprised at what she was telling him. But it seemed so natural, lying within his arms, telling him these things, she suddenly realized.

He hugged her. "Maybe that's why you write, because it's easier to put down how you feel on paper?"

She stared at him. "How did you know?"

"Haven't I been telling you that I know you?" he teased.

"Shane? Know me. All of me," she begged. "Please?"

He drew in his breath sharply. "Jaclyn, be sure you know what you're saying," he warned. "Be very, very sure."

"I was sure when I came up here," she said softly.

"I'm not . . ." His voice was unsteady. "But I can't let that stop me, Jaclyn, because I want you so very badly!"

His mouth met hers, and their arms closed about each other, shutting out all doubt. It was her body, but when his lips and hands touched her breasts, the softness between legs that parted for him, she found he was showing her a side of her she hadn't known existed, a warm, passionate side.

When she gasped aloud, surprised at the response his touch ignited, she discovered a dimension of his personality she'd only glimpsed lately, too, when he stopped, worried that he had hurt her. He was tender initiating her into the art of lovemaking, but by then his caresses had asked, not demanded, a response, and she pulled him closer, unwilling to let his fear—or hers—stop them. The search, the knowing, must be complete, she vowed, and trusting and eager, Shane and Jaclyn broke the last barrier.

When she cried out at the pain, his movements slowed, and he covered her mouth with reassuring kisses and loving words until she became aware of a spreading warmth and a throbbing need for him. For a moment it startled her into stillness, then her body began moving with him, against him, around him.

"Oh, Jaclyn," he moaned, his lips against her ear. "You incredible, beautiful woman. I love you."

For the moment she thought she had imagined him saying it, then neither could speak as their bodies continued the knowing, a tantalizing, tormenting journey, spiraling to a peak of splintering ecstasy. She cried out in wonder at the exquisite sensations sweeping through her. Shane's movements quickened, then with a hoarse cry he knew his release.

Gathering her in his arms, Shane drew in a satisfied sigh. "And I thought Lady Luck had forgotten me," he said quietly.

Jaclyn shivered convulsively. Why did the thought of that world have to intrude now? she thought bitterly.

"Cold?" He drew the sheets up around them.

She shook her head. She wasn't lying. The chill was from within.

"Did I hurt you?"

"No."

They lay staring up at the stars through the skylight. Listening to the sound of his breathing returning to normal, wrapped in his arms and the afterglow of their passion, she felt a bittersweet longing for the moment to last.

Seize it, she told herself. This may be the only time you'll be like this with this man. When reason takes over again and you remember why you can't love him, and he forgets those words of love spoken in passion . . .

He pulled her over so that she was lying on top of him. "Tell me that you love me as much as I love you."

A lump formed in her throat, constricting it, and she couldn't breathe, couldn't speak.

"Jaclyn?" His voice was urgent, questioning.

"I do, Shane, I do!" The pent-up words were out.

Uttering an exultant cry, he brought her face down to his, kissing her almost fiercely. Then he was drawing away from her lips, reaching up to touch the wetness on her cheeks.

"You're crying! I *did* hurt you!"

"No!" She shook her head, and her hair swished across his chest, long strands glinting like silver under the moonlight. "No, I—I can't explain it, but you didn't hurt me, honestly."

He held her close, pressing her head against his shoulder, stroking her hair. Lulled by the motion of his hands, the comfort of his body warm next to hers, she felt her tension easing. She wanted to find some way to explain her tears, but she couldn't think of a way to do it. Listening to the gentle wash of the sea upon the shore outside, she found the need to explain less and less important as time passed and he didn't press her for an explanation.

Later she woke, troubled, and it took a moment to realize the roaring noise wasn't from race cars, from the familiar nightmare, but from the crash of thunder and the sea tossing below. Rain slid in sparkling sheets down the skylight glass, splashing shimmering patterns across the face and shoulders of the man who slept beside her. The man who had said he loved her.

He stirred, opened his eyes, and looked at her. "Jaclyn? What's wrong? Not another nightmare!"

"No. The thunder woke me." And, after a moment, she said, "Shane, I should go now."

"Shh," he murmured, pressing his lips against hers, parting them with his tongue. His hands moved over her again, caressing, urgent, and passion flowed between them once more.

She explored his body with her hands, tentatively at first, then, emboldened by the ardor of his response, their exploration went further, and she felt her desire heighten to an unbearable pitch. They came together in a moment lit by the electric brilliance of lightning flashing overhead, then from within—a climax wild and tempestuous as the night storm. As the storm moved out to sea Jaclyn stayed with Shane in his arms and slept again.

CHAPTER NINE

They woke to sunlight filling the room, the cries of sea gulls, the sound of the surf.

"So you weren't a dream." Shane smiled as he leaned over to kiss her. "Hey, don't get all shy again," he said as she blushed and pulled the sheet higher.

"I'm not used to waking up in bed with a man," she told him wryly. Or, she thought, seeing a man in the nude, as he swung his legs over the side of the bed and stretched.

He laughed as he tossed her the robe she had worn the night before. "You'll have to get used to it. Hungry?"

She nodded a little uncertainly, wondering what he had meant by saying she'd have to get used to it. Sliding her hands under the heavy fall of her hair, she lifted it outside the collar of the robe in a graceful motion.

Shane, busy tying the belt of another robe, stopped to stare at her.

"Why are you looking at me like that?" she asked, disconcerted.

He came to wrap his arms around her. "With the sun in your hair, you look good enough for breakfast, golden girl. If missing dinner for you was a good idea"—this said with a mischievous leer—"perhaps I'll skip breakfast, too."

Jaclyn laughed as she put her hands on his shoulders to stop him. "Please, I need something a little more substantial than love this morning."

His eyes glinted silver in the sunlight as he stared down at her. Her heart missed a beat at his disbelieving smile, then he took her hand, and she ran down the stairs with him, her steps as light as her heart this morning.

Downstairs, they moved around the kitchen, getting breakfast, at ease with each other. We're acting like we do this every day, like two old married people, Jaclyn thought, watching Shane scramble eggs as she set out coffee cups on a tray.

But we're not, she reminded herself harshly, and she frowned. He'd said nothing about marriage, but it could never be, never, not while he raced—

"Something wrong?" Shane interrupted her thoughts.

She shook her head. "Coffee's ready."

They ate on the balcony, Shane wolfing down two helpings of eggs and bacon and four pieces of toast before he seemed full.

"Coffee?"

He nodded, and she lifted the coffeepot, the sleeve of the robe sliding back, revealing a slender wrist and the line of her graceful arm. With the other hand she flicked a strand of hair that fell against her cheek, and then reached across to pick up his cup. Her lashes were gold-tipped fans against her cheeks as she watched the dark brown liquid fill the cup, and her nose wrinkled pleasurably at the steam rising from it.

Jaclyn looked up, and her eyes were a sparkling emerald, clear and direct as the ocean before them. Her lips curved into a smile.

"Cream?" she asked, setting down the pot.

"Is there any left?" he responded with a grin. "You look like a kitten who's licked it all up."

Her eyes twinkled merrily as she poured it in a thick, ivory stream into the coffee. "Here." She held the cup with both hands, proferring it like something precious.

He took it and watched as she lifted the spoon from a small jar of honey and held a piece of toast close to it. Holding the spoon high, she watched the honey catch the sunlight and turn it into an amber jewel that flowed slowly, so slowly, onto the toast. The tip of her tongue touched her upper lip as she savored the delicious sight, anticipating it, leaning forward to perch at the edge of her chair. The golden mass fell in heavy, rolling drops that moved languidly onto the bread, glinting as she tilted it so that the sweet mass covered the dry surface. Then the spoon was dropped into the jar, and it sank down into the golden depths before she turned her attention to the toast. Bringing the toast to her lips, her eyes at first opened wide, then closed in pleasure as she bit down and enclosed it in her mouth. Chewing slowly, appreciatively, she opened her eyes and tossed her head, and her hair blew out in golden strands the color of the honey in the salty breeze from the ocean. Her mouth moved from side to side, her cheek filling then concaving gently as her teeth crunched the contrast of hard toast and syrupy sweetness, then she swallowed. The tip of her tongue emerged again to lick tentatively the glistening drops of stickiness from the curving line of her lips with a languid motion.

Just as she was about to take another bite, she looked up and was surprised to see a look of desire in Shane's eyes.

"Is something the matter?" she asked innocently.

He shook his head, his expression becoming one of disbelief.

"Why were you looking at me like that?"

"I was just thinking that you eat like you do everything else," he said, almost musingly. "Slowly, sensuously. I think I was in love with you from the moment you walked into the speedway—sleek, long-legged, moving like a graceful cat. Your hair was blowing wild and free in the wind like it is now, and I had eyes for nothing but you."

The corners of her mouth lifted. "Don't you remember how we fought?"

He shook his head. "No, I couldn't do anything but stare at you then. It was only later that things got mixed up. Anyway, never mind that now," he said, leaning across the table, drawing her forward with his hand at her neck, their lips meeting.

"Mmm," he murmured appreciatively when he released her lips and licked his. "You taste as sweet as you look. Have you had enough?" he asked, pulling her to her feet. "I want to feast my eyes on you again, honey-lips."

"Shane, let me get the dishes in," she protested.

But he was drawing her inside, upstairs to his bed again. And nothing would persuade him—or her, she had to admit—from doing it again as they loved and talked and laughed and loved again until late into the afternoon.

Jaclyn slipped from the bed when Shane slept. She stood, studying his face, relaxed in sleep, the scar showing white as his black hair waved back from his forehead, revealing it. His shoulders and torso were bronze against the stark white of the sheets, the lower half of the perfect male beauty of his body hidden beneath.

Closing her eyes against the tears that threatened to fall, she wrapped her arms around herself. She couldn't have him, and she had let herself fall in love with him! Her love was as dangerous as those fast cars he raced, as certain to cause her pain as the metal lover to which he gave his passion.

It would be like having half a man, when she wanted a whole one, one who loved her with no mistress, real or metal, to steal his love—or his life. And his film work—wasn't that another passion that would take even more of him from her? Would there be enough of him left for her, even if he wanted her?

A sob rose in her throat, and she slipped quickly from the room, afraid she'd wake him and he'd ask why she was crying.

Her tears mingled with the spray in the shower. The rushing water drowned out the sound of her sobs. When she won control of her feelings, she reached for the soap, then dropped it when the shower door opened.

"So this is where you went," Shane said, stepping inside.

"W-what are you doing?" she spluttered, surprised.

"I thought you might need some help scrubbing your back," he said calmly. But his eyes were alight with mischief. He pulled her to him, closing her in his arms, and nuzzled at her wet neck. The water pulsed down on their bodies.

"You're helping me?" she retorted, laughing.

He bent for the soap, worked up a lather in his hands, and told her to turn around. Spreading the lather across her back, he massaged it into her skin, slowly, sensuously, caressing more than cleaning, his hands more pleasurable, more erotic, as they traveled down her body. Then he was turning her around, and his thumbs traced circles with the soap on her breasts, her stomach, and the slightly sore place that he had been the first to excite with his sensual explorations.

"Jaclyn?"

She slid her arms around him and pressed her face against his chest. "Mmm?"

"Move in with me?"

"What?"

"You heard me. Move in with me. Don't leave like you'd planned, and we'll—"

"No!" she said sharply, drawing back. "I—I can't, Shane."

"You didn't let me finish," he complained mildly. "I didn't mean it would be permanent."

"I don't want to have an affair with you," she said. Opening the shower door, she stepped out and found a towel, keeping her face averted so that he couldn't see the expression of pain on her face.

"Wait a minute. You don't mean you're going to fly back to New York, as though nothing has happened between us, do you?" There was disbelief in his voice. "Look, I'm not doing this well," he said, stepping out and wrapping a towel around his waist. "Bear with me. Maybe I should have brought a script. What I'm trying to do, in my own clumsy way, is propose, darling."

"No."

"What?"

"I said no. I can't marry you, Shane," she said quietly. "Why?"

She stared at him, saw his confusion. But how could she explain when she couldn't understand herself right now?

"I'm not the sort of woman who expects something because you took me to bed."

"Don't talk like that!" He took her by the shoulders,

194

shook her lightly. "That's not why I'm asking, and you know it. We love each other."

He'd said it when they made love, but she'd thought it a promise made in passion, and took it as such even now.

"You love me?"

"Yes! You know I do," he insisted. "My God, I've known what was going to happen from the moment we met. You did, too. You had to. Last night, today, only proved it."

"What did it prove?"

"Until last night I couldn't really be sure that you weren't reacting to the fact that Gino was involved in the accident at the race. You could have been upset that he might be hurt."

"What on earth are you talking about?"

"The pictures. Wait, I'll get them." Puzzled, she watched as he left the room and returned with a pile of black-and-white photographs in his hand.

Curious, Jaclyn took them, and when she looked at the top picture, her eyes widened with shock. There, in stark tableau, she was pictured with her face a frozen mask of horror, caught by the camera's unblinking eye. She put it down, forced herself to pick up the next, in which Luigi was slapping her, and the next and the next, knowing now what they recorded without having to look at another.

"Where—where did you get these?" she managed to ask, her lips trembling.

"A reporter I know brought them to the hospital. He thought I might be interested in them," Shane said dryly.

"So you've had them all this time." She stared down at the pile of paper printed with those damning images. Those pictures said so much, she thought. "Why did you wait so long to show them to me? What point were you going to make?"

Shane shook his head slowly. "No point, Jaclyn. They just told me something you couldn't put into words: that you care about me. Why are you holding back? What do you want, Jaclyn? I don't understand you today."

"I don't want anything! Does every woman who sleeps with you expect something the next day?" she flung at him a little desperately.

"Jaclyn!" His tone, his look, was warning.

"I'm—sorry. I didn't mean that. But I don't want anything. No, I do. I want to go back to the hotel now, please."

"Not until we get this settled."

Jaclyn rubbed at her forehead. It was beginning to ache from tension. "I wish you'd just go away so I could think," she muttered. "Oh, what am I saying? This is your house. I'll go."

"Dressed like that?" Shane attempted to bring some levity into the tenseness that hung between them, heavy like the approaching storm that she could see in the gathering darkness outside. "Stay here, and I'll bring up your clothes."

He returned with them and lingered in the bathroom until he saw that she wanted to dress in privacy. With a sigh, he left the room, shutting the door behind him.

Jaclyn pulled on her clothes quickly. Dragging a comb through her hair, she stared at herself in the mirror. Her reflection was that of a woman who looked even more vulnerable than yesterday, when she'd dressed in Shane's robe while she waited for her clothes to dry and had caught a glimpse of herself in another mirror. Wasn't a woman supposed to look happy, fulfilled, after making love with a man she loved? She only felt confused, unhappy, and it showed. Sighing, she went downstairs.

Shane turned at the sound of her footsteps on the stairs. "Let's sit down and try to sort this out, Jaclyn."

"No, please. Not here. Not now. I—" She shook her head, at a loss for words, and found her hands nervously drawing her jacket across her chest in a defensive gesture.

"Where, then?" He looked slightly exasperated. "You know, I won't attack you, Jaclyn," he teased her gently.

"You wouldn't have to," she said, miserable.

"I'll take you for a drive, then."

"It's raining."

"I don't mind driving in the rain."

She nodded. "I'll get my things," she said, walking over to pick up her tape recorder and notes.

"Leave them, we'll be back. No, forget it. Take them if it makes you happy," he said, throwing up his hands when he saw her look of apprehension.

She bent to pick up the book she had been leafing through the night before, the one that had set off the nightmare.

"Give that to me. I'll put it away," Shane said.

His voice startled her, and she realized that she had been staring at the picture again. Shane took the book, glancing at it as he began to close it, then stopped as his attention was arrested. Long moments passed as she watched him read the paragraph beneath the picture. Then he looked up, his expression one of surprise, then understanding, and of—sympathy?

"My God, that's it!" he said. "The whole puzzle's beginning to fall into place. That's what's been bothering you, isn't it? That you fell in love with someone you're afraid will get killed like your father?"

"Yes—no, I mean, I don't know. I'm so mixed up right now. Everything's just moving too fast."

"Jaclyn, we have to talk about this."

"No! You'll never understand. No one does. I don't even understand the way I feel about it sometimes. Right now everything's just moving too fast," she repeated.

"It's because I didn't want you to go back to New York. Otherwise I'd have waited to propose, Jaclyn."

"I have to, Shane. I have to sort out how I feel. We met just two weeks ago!"

"But we know how we feel. What does the amount of time matter?"

"Can we go now, please?" she asked, her voice rising a little in desperation. She couldn't bear any more questions, any more torment.

He shoved his hands in his pockets and studied her, his black eyebrows drawn together in a frown. Finally he nodded. "I'll get my wallet," he said, turning to climb the stairs to his bedroom. "Maybe when you calm down, when you're alone and you think about it—"

The doorbell rang, jangling the tenseness between them, an interruption as harsh and startling as the lightning that suddenly streaked across the sky. Jaclyn jumped.

"Now, who can that be?" Shane muttered as he moved past her to answer it.

"Where is she, Jaeger?" Gino stood in the doorway, his handsome face contorted with fury. "I've been watching the house, so don't try to tell me she isn't here!" He pushed past Shane and strode into the room.

"Gino! I thought you were in Italy." Jaclyn moved toward him. She stopped when she saw his expression.

"It served my purpose that you thought that." His fists clenched and unclenched at his sides. "I thought that this interview business was no more than an excuse for him to lure you into his bed, and I was right!"

"Look, Spinnelli, you can't come barging in here like this and talk like that to Jaclyn," Shane warned.

"He didn't lure me, Gino," she said quietly.

"Are you saying you stayed the night and didn't go to bed with him?" Gino's voice was ugly with accusation.

"He didn't lure me," she repeated. "I love him!" Her words were out before she really knew what she was saying, surprising both men—and herself.

Something flickered across Gino's face, so quickly there, and then gone, that Jaclyn blinked, wondering if it was the lightning that changed Gino into someone frightening. Shane, standing behind him, didn't see it.

"Damn you, Jaeger!" Gino spun around, swinging his fist up at a startled Shane.

With the instinct born of his film roles, Shane ducked, and the blow went astray. Enraged, Gino threw himself at Shane and the two went sprawling to the floor, knocking over the coffee table.

"Stop it, stop it!" Jaclyn cried, horrified, as they rained blows on each other.

Shane staggered to his feet, looking dazed. A trickle of blood dripped from the corner of his mouth.

Gino leaped to his feet, lashing out with his fists, connecting with Shane's jaw. Jaclyn watched him jerk away, time seeming to freeze, as if the scene were in slow motion. It was like watching one of Shane's films. Only this was no movie, no stunt man for a double—this was real life!

He wasn't winning, either, like he did in those Westerns, she began to realize as Gino's attack became more vicious. Shane's movements were slower; he was tiring more than Gino as he tried to defend himself. When he shook his head again, and then again, Jaclyn remembered the migraine he'd suffered the day before from the head injury he'd so recently suffered.

"Please, Gino, you've got to stop! You'll kill him!"

She grabbed at Gino's arm, tried to prevent him from landing another blow, but he only shook her off. Flesh met flesh again in a sickening smack as Gino's fist smashed against Shane's jaw, and Shane fell to his knees.

She had to get help, before one of them killed the other. But where? Shane had no telephone, and there were no houses on either side of his. Wait, she thought, there's a telephone down the block. She ran from the room, down the stairs, and out into the night, sobbing.

The rain had begun again, and its coolness startled, then chilled her. Down the driveway she ran, her feet slipping, tears blinding her. She glanced over her shoulder and saw headlights flash on and move toward her. Gino was coming after her!

Quickly she stepped off the sidewalk and ran across the road, her only thought to move to the other side of the street. A bright beam of light sliced across her path, and she was caught in a clash of headlights from both sides. Stopping in midflight, she looked about frantically, not knowing where to run to get out of the way.

A horn blared, tires screeched, and a car was coming at her, sliding on the rain-slicked road in an awful, deadly slowness that seemed unreal.

She couldn't move, and then she *was* moving, being lifted into the air as the car's bumper caught her on the hip and flung her with relentless momentum to the side of the road. She landed on the hard, wet pavement with a force that brought blinding pain, then blackness.

She came to moments later, hearing someone shouting

her name. Everything hurt. One knee throbbed painfully, and her head ached alarmingly.

"Jaclyn—please, God—are you all right?" Shane shouted hoarsely. His face hovered over hers. He ran a hand, which trembled, across her forehead, smoothing back her rain-wet hair.

She stared at him, blinking in the rain that was falling gently, too stunned to answer him.

"I couldn't stop! She ran right into my path! It was an accident!" a woman's voice cried shrilly, defensively.

Jaclyn tried to raise herself to reassure the woman, but the world spun.

"Lie back, don't move!" Concern made Shane's voice harsh. He gathered her hands in his, felt the chill that was already seeping into her body from the pavement.

"Stay with her!" he commanded the driver, who stood above Jaclyn, wringing her hands. He returned with a blanket from his car and covered Jaclyn in an ineffectual attempt to ward off the rain and chill.

More cars stopped now, and the faces of concerned strangers gathered around to peer down at her. Someone offered to call an ambulance and the police, and Shane nodded without taking his eyes from her face.

"I'll be all right, Shane," she told him, knowing it wasn't altogether true. She hurt so badly that she was sure she'd never move again. But she was alive, and now that the full impact of what could have happened hit her, she began shaking with reaction as well as cold.

"Where do you hurt?"

"Where don't I?" she wanted to quip, but she didn't dare. Shane was upset enough. And she'd really never felt less like joking.

"It's only my knee," she lied between her teeth, clenching them as much to bear the pain as to stop them from chattering. "Please, Shane, just help me up and take me to the hotel. I don't want to go to the hospital."

"I don't care what you want, you're going!" Glancing up, he scanned the street. "Where the hell is that ambulance?" he muttered worriedly, taking her hands in his again to rub some warmth into them.

"What happened to Gino?"

"Out cold," Shane told her in a grim voice. "When you ran from the house it distracted him for just a second, and that was long enough for me to finally make a good blow."

"Shane, shouldn't you make sure he's all right?"

"When I've made certain that you are. And not until!" He raised his head to search for the ambulance again.

"Aren't you—?" The woman driver stepped forward hesitantly, staring at Shane in the glare from the overhead streetlight. "Aren't you Shane Jaeger, the actor?"

"What the hell does it matter at a time like this? Oh, hell, I'm sorry, Jaclyn," he said when she squeezed his hands so that he had to look at her and see the silent appeal in her eyes. "But what am I supposed to say, 'Yes, ma'am, and how many autographs today?' "

Later he stood at the foot of her hospital bed and said he'd apologized for his behavior to the woman, hours later, it felt to Jaclyn, after she'd been examined and X-rayed and forced, by the doctor and Shane, into spending the night there.

She sat in her bed, staring at her immobile left leg, clad in a ridiculous-looking thing that resembled a corset. If she had only a minor fracture of the knee, then why did she need this ridiculous contraption? she asked herself despairingly. She was trying to decide whether to laugh or cry, and about to do both, when she realized Shane stood in the doorway. Grabbing up the sheets to cover the shape-less hospital gown, she'd been painfully reminded of the bruises that made her body ache in a thousand places as she lay back against the pillows.

"Jaclyn?" Shane walked into the room and stood at the end of her bed, his face dark and unreadable in the dimly lit room. "How are you feeling?" he asked when she didn't answer, pulling a chair up beside her bed. His voice was gentle.

"Too well to be here," she snapped.

He sighed. "Look, Jaclyn, please try to understand. I know you don't want to stay the night. But you said your head hurt, and the doctor wants to make sure you haven't suffered a concussion."

"My head feels fine." She jerked her head back to glare at him, wincing as she did so.

"Next you'll tell me your knee isn't hurting you, ei-ther," he mocked. He leaned back in the chair and studied her. "You can't get up and run away from me now, and it's frustrating you, isn't it?"

"Oh, please, go away, Shane," she said dully. The strain of the scene in his house, and the accident, was beginning to catch up with her.

"If I leave, will you promise to try to get some sleep?"

"Don't tell me what to do!" Her voice came out sharper than she meant it to.

But it didn't bother him. "I'm glad to see your being tossed by that car didn't knock the fight out of you." Getting up from the chair, he approached the side of her bed and bent to touch her cheek. One side of her face had been grazed when she fell to the street. "Poor face. First one side, now the other," he said, referring to the time her cheek had been bruised the day Luigi had slapped her at

203

the race. "We're going to have to talk about it, Jaclyn, when you get out of here."

"I don't want to talk about it. Ever! Now, please, will you go away?" she cried, turning to bury her face in her pillow.

"Jaclyn—"

"I'm afraid you'll have to go now, Mr. Jaeger," a stern voice interrupted. "The young lady needs some rest."

"But—" he began.

"Sorry," was the blunt rejoinder of the nurse who had entered the room.

Shane sighed. "Good night, Jaclyn. I'll be back in the morning to see you." He bent to kiss her, but stopped and slowly straightened when she turned her head away.

The nurse marched forward after Shane had left, offering a painkiller for the leg, and, before she left the room, showing Jaclyn how to operate the television with a remote control device beside the bed. "Might take your mind off the pain till the pill works," she said with gruff sympathy.

Nothing will do that—or take my mind off the ache I feel inside, Jaclyn thought, pushing the "on" button. A detective show didn't interest her, neither did a sports program nor a situation comedy.

On one channel a movie was playing, one with a familiar title, and Shane's face suddenly appeared on the screen, startling Jaclyn into believing he'd walked back into the room, the picture was so sharp and real-looking. He was dressed in a checked shirt and a leather vest, with form-hugging jeans tucked into dusty cowboy boots, and Jaclyn watched him take off his Stetson and wave it. A feminine figure ran across a prairie toward him. A look of anticipation was in his eyes, almost silver in the bright sunlight, just as Jaclyn had seen them, his mouth curving in that sensual smile so familiar to her. Jaclyn watched, experiencing a curious pain as Shane lifted the woman into his strong arms, holding her close. Then he was swinging her up and around in a movement of pure joy. The film's background music swelled in a beat of the old West, the sounds of a country fiddle and a banjo increasing the excitement as Shane lowered the woman to her feet and his mouth claimed hers.

Jaclyn tore her eyes from the picture, her head throbbing with the sudden movement, a tightness in her chest hurting even more. Remembering that this was the actress who'd vilified Shane as a "dictator" on the set—and that Shane despised the woman in return—didn't help when the two made such convincing lovers on the screen. And then Jaclyn remembered the way Shane had been with her, how she'd become one of his women.

How, she thought miserably, pushing the "off" button of the remote control device, did you really know when the actor wasn't acting?

It wasn't the first time she'd asked herself this. But it would be the last. She'd done what she'd said she wouldn't do—gotten involved with him. Now she had to pick up the pieces and get back to New York and the new life she'd made for herself in the last few years.

CHAPTER TEN

"I thought we were saying good night, not good-bye," a familiar voice said coldly.

"Shane!" Jaclyn gasped. "I—I didn't see you." She'd been moving slowly across the infield of the racetrack on her crutches, cautious of grass made slippery by a chilly April shower, thankful that the place was nearly deserted, so that her leg wouldn't be bumped.

His presence was totally unexpected, when she'd been told to meet him in the pit section. He'd approached her quietly, seeming to come upon her as stealthily as the panther he resembled in his jet-black driver's suit. Was it the silver streak of trim around the neckband that made his eyes look so metallic-gray with anger? she asked herself, shivering a little. Jaclyn's slight movement caused her to lose her balance, already precarious on the wet grass. She felt herself slipping. His hand shot out and clutched her arm, steadying her. Once Jaclyn got her balance on the crutches, she raised her eyes to thank him. But there was an expression of—disgust?—on his face, as if he hadn't wanted to touch her but had been forced to. Then it was replaced by a cold mask. They stared at each other for a time that ticked by like an eternity, then Jaclyn looked away.

In the weeks since she'd checked herself out of the hospital the morning after the accident, flying home without saying good-bye to him, she'd wondered what it would be like to meet him again. Writing about him after what he'd come to mean to her had been hell, when she'd had to disattach herself emotionally at the same time and listen to the tapes to check her facts. The sound of his voice on them had brought back the memories of their time together at Daytona. It was a wonder her typewriter hadn't rusted after all the times she'd put her head down on it and cried. Now, after all the hours of writing—and crying—dreaming of him, even thinking she'd seen him as she and Gino came out of the church where her mother had just been married the other day, now she'd been forced to meet him here at a New York racetrack. When would the pain stop? she thought despairingly.

"I'm all right," she told him when he asked how she was, but still he didn't release her. His fingers hurt, a vise around the tender flesh. But his touch was sending a warmth up her arm that spread through her body, making her tremble. His frown, the way he let her go abruptly, told her he'd misunderstood her reaction, that he thought her shiver was because she found his touch distasteful.

"How did Gino like his little idyll broken up?" His voice was harsh. "I tried to get in touch with your publisher after—after the other day, but it was too late. I'm surprised Gino would let you see *me* again under the circumstances."

Jaclyn shook her head, confused at Shane's disjointed speech, staring at the expression that looked like pain crossing his face. What was he talking about?

"Where is he?" he asked abruptly, before she could ask him anything. "You did bring the photographer. From

Life-Styles magazine." When she nodded he asked, "Not *Star Gaze?*"

Her face flamed. That was the gossip magazine she'd contacted when she'd been angry at his forcing her to interview him. How had he found out? she wondered, studying his face intently for some sign of anger. But his face was devoid of expression; the faintest lifting of one corner of his mouth almost made her think he was about to smile.

"I didn't sell it to them," she said quickly. "I never really meant to. Why did you insist on my coming here, telling the publisher you wouldn't agree to pictures for the article without me being present? It—wasn't for the pictures, was it? You want to—" She trailed off, not sure anymore of *what* she thought was the reason for her presence today.

"To punish you for leaving like that? Is that what you think?" His voice was harsh. "It never occurred to you that—"

"Hey, Shane, there you are!" a race official called as he approached them. "Got a little matter here I need you for." He gestured at the clipboard he carried.

Grimacing, Shane dug in his pocket, then held out a key to Jaclyn. "Here, you go on to my camper. Rest that leg. I'll be there in a minute."

She hesitated, then took it, deciding that if they had some privacy, perhaps they could get the whole thing over with. At least the other man had had the decency not to smirk, she thought gratefully as she started for the camper.

"Jaclyn! Heard you were comin'. Are you lookin' for Shane?"

She glanced up and saw Mitch's familiar rough-hewn

face grinning at her. Smiling warily, she greeted him and explained where she was headed. What, she wondered, had Shane told the man about her when she'd left Daytona so quickly?

"Take you there myself," he was saying. "Real sorry you had to get back to New York so sudden. Didn't get to say good-bye to you, and all."

"I—I'm sorry, Mitch. It was one of those last-minute things."

"Yeah, so Shane said. Leg gonna be okay?"

She nodded, keeping her eyes fixed on the ground. They walked in silence for a few minutes, Mitch slowing his stride to match her halting progress.

"Are you sure you're okay?" He peered at her, frowning, his eyes worried. "I hope—that is, I know this probably ain't none of my business, but I reckon I gotta ask—"

"Look, Mitch." Jaclyn rushed to stop him. "I'm only here today to get some pictures."

"And so you can snap my head off like Shane does," Mitch finished without missing a beat. He grinned, unabashed, then his expression became serious. "Now, that's too bad. Me and Maggie—you know, my wife—well, we were kinda hopin' otherwise. Shane did try to tell me you were interested in that Italian fellow. Said something about a wedding.'

Jaclyn swallowed the lump that had risen in her throat and tried to walk a little faster, so Mitch wouldn't see the tears in her eyes. For a moment she considered a correction about Gino. Then she reconsidered. Better for him to think that; it made things easier.

Was it the mention of Gino that made her think she saw him appear before her? Jaclyn blinked, then the man was hurrying past, and she wasn't so sure. She shook her head, telling herself she was imagining things. Maybe it was just that man who'd been in Shane's pit at Daytona. After all, Gino's stopover in New York had ended the day after the wedding.

"Watch where you're goin' there, honey," Mitch warned, reaching out a hand to stabilize her. "Shucks, there I went and got some grease on you!"

She stopped and watched him ineffectually rub at the spot on her jacket with a handkerchief that looked as if it had been used for the same purpose several times already that day.

"Occupational hazard, I keep tellin' Maggie." He laughed a little, following her gaze to his hands. "Never quite get the stuff out from beneath the fingernails, not if you keep a hand in it, as most of us mechanics seem to do."

"But you were a driver."

"One of them who couldn't resist helpin' here and there, if I thought I knew better." Not like those new drivers, he seemed to imply.

Come to think of it, Jaclyn realized she'd never seen Shane or Gino do anything beneath the hood. Again, unbidden, that mechanic's hands came to mind, the one back at Daytona, the one she'd just seen. His hands were clean then, she remembered, because she'd bumped into him, and when he had grasped her arm instinctively to right her, she'd looked down, and his hands hadn't left an imprint like Mitch's.

"There you go. Sure you're comfortable?" Mitch was asking as he helped her up into the camper. "How 'bout somethin' to prop up that leg? No? Then I'll be seein' if Maggie is here yet. Said she didn't want to get here hours early, like me and Shane. You'll be sittin' with us, won't you?"

"I—I was going to leave right after the pictures, Mitch."

He eyed her strangely. "Now, that seems a waste, don't it? Sure you won't stick around? No? Then I guess I'll be sayin' good-bye."

Jaclyn nodded. "Mitch? Thanks for—implying you wished Shane and I could have worked it out. That was sweet of you."

"Just the truth," he said gruffly. "Didn't mean to be pokin' my nose in, but that Shane, he's like a son to me. And I thought he'd found a woman who's natural, down to earth, like my Maggie, to make him happy. Oh, hell, there I go makin' you uncomfortable again."

"Mitch? I—" she began, then stopped. Forget it, she told herself. "Good-bye, Mitch. And thanks."

"Sure thing, honey," he said, tipping his Stetson before he left her.

Like a son, he'd said. How nice, she thought, looking around at the paneled walls of the camper. She'd known the bond of affection was strong between the two men, but Mitch's words had shown that even more so. And Mitch thought highly of her, too. But what he wanted, what she'd wanted, couldn't be!

What would her life have been like if they had gotten married, Jaclyn asked herself, sighing. I'd be traveling around with him, watching while he worked on a film, or raced at a track, she answered herself. Oh, that wasn't literally true, she knew. He admired and supported her work, he'd said so. And she could do it anywhere. She loved the traveling, even seeing different places, meeting people, as she had with her parents.

What about sitting at a racetrack like this one, always wondering if this was going to be the race? . . .

I wouldn't even mind that, she thought. Once, she'd thought she couldn't bear that. Now, when she knew otherwise, when she knew she loved him, she knew she could bear anything to be with him. But it wasn't possible!

Gino had tried to change her mind about it, she remembered. But she hadn't loved Gino enough to put herself through that pain. She remembered the difficulty she'd had in convincing Gino it didn't matter what he did, it was Shane she loved. Funny, that was the second time she'd thought of Gino that day, she thought. Maybe it was because Mitch had mentioned him, or maybe that crew member who reminded her of him.

The minutes ticked past, and Jaclyn fidgeted, uneasy with waiting for Shane and what he wanted to say, uncomfortable with the leg—and edgy with where her thoughts were leading.

Strange that the man hadn't been in the film she'd seen later of the Daytona race, in the pits with Shane's crew, when they were interviewed just after his crash. But he could have been in the background, or not asked to help on the crew that day. But at Daytona she saw him only just before the crash, not earlier, during the days of practice, or after. She'd come to know many of the crew members, not just of the Spinnelli crew, but of other cars as well, since she spent so much time at the racetrack.

How had Sophia liked her interview? Jaclyn wondered. Before Gino flew back she had given him copies of the magazine it had appeared in, and he'd promised to give them to his sister. She hadn't heard anything yet. Was it that Sophia hadn't liked it enough to call? Or was it that Gino's business in New York had taken longer than he expected, and he'd flown back later than she thought? He'd told her not to bother coming to the airport with him to see him off, since her leg was difficult to get around on.

It was bothering her now, the leg, she realized. She got to her feet and opened the door, looking out for Shane. There were few people on the scene yet, the race still hours away. Some crew members milled about. There was that man in black again, the one who resembled Gino, dressed in the same black uniform—one of Shane's crew?

Jaclyn found herself hopping down awkwardly from the camper, curious when the man in black always seemed to put his head down as people walked past him. When he entered the garage—stealthily, she thought—Jaclyn followed him slowly on her crutches.

Black-clad legs were visible beneath a car painted with Shane's name on its black-and-silver door. When the man slid from beneath it on a dolly, reaching for a wrench, Jaclyn gasped. It was Gino!

"What are you doing here? What are you doing to Shane's car?" She backed away, eyes wide with horror. *He* was the one who'd tampered with Shane's car before—she was sure of it now!

"Come back here, Jaclyn," Gino persuaded softly.

But her feet kept moving backward, and all the while her lips couldn't form words, and her eyes stayed on that wrench in his hands.

"Gino! Get back!" a voice ordered.

Shane!

Jaclyn turned. "Oh, Shane, he was trying to do something to your car!" she cried.

"Never mind the car now. Get outside, Jaclyn."

"Yes, the hell with the car," Gino agreed, advancing on

213

Shane with the wrench raised in his hand. His eyes glittered with hatred.

"Outside, Jaclyn," Shane repeated.

"Gino, put it down, before someone gets hurt," she begged. "Please, don't blame Shane for—"

Shane grabbed at her arm, pushing her roughly toward the garage door. "He's past reasoning with, can't you see that? Get outside, before you get hurt!"

"No, Shane, let me talk to— Gino, no!" she screamed when the Italian took advantage of Shane's attention on her to swing at him with the wrench. It barely missed Shane's head.

Sobbing now with fear, and pain from forcing her leg along too quickly, Jaclyn measured the distance to the door with her eyes, and in her heart she knew Shane might be badly hurt before she got help. She looked back, horrified, to see Shane slipping on a patch of grease on the floor and losing his balance, sliding, sliding, and Gino bending to pick up something long and heavy—a length of pipe! Jaclyn screamed a warning, but Shane's movements looked so slow and Gino's so quick, raising the pipe!

There was no time now! Jaclyn cast about for something to throw, then found her hand tightening around the crutch in her right hand, throwing it with all her might.

It caught Gino at the knees, and then he was falling, striking his head with an awful sound on the cement.

Uttering a cry of pain as her injured leg tried to take all her weight and couldn't, Jaclyn fell.

"Are you all right?" It was Shane who bent over her to ask. "No, lie still. Gino's out cold. Did you hurt yourself when you fell? Your leg? No, don't move. I'll get the doctor—"

"*Shane!* I'm okay, really," she interrupted him. "Just a

little out of breath. And the floor's so cold! Help me up, please, before I catch pneumonia!" But he bent and lifted her in his arms.

"Put me down!"

"It really rankles you that you have to submit to me holding you, doesn't it?" His smile was sardonic. "It would him, too, if he could see it." He jerked his head in the direction of the still-prone Gino.

"What happened?" A uniformed police officer hurried toward them.

"Where were you?" Shane demanded. "Weren't you supposed to be watching the entrance to the garage?"

"Mix-up, sir. Apparently a kid was bribed to get my attention away from it. I'll be right here now, don't worry."

"Who's worrying? The lady got him. He's inside. You won't be needing that," he told the officer when the man drew his gun.

Jaclyn shivered, and Shane held her closer. She could feel his strong, steady heartbeat and hoped he couldn't feel hers pounding madly against him.

"I'll have you out of the wind in a minute."

"Where are you taking me?"

"To the infield hospital. Hey, Bill, grab the crutches back there and follow me, hear?"

She protested, but it did no good. When he put her down it was just where he'd made up his mind to take her. She glared at him. "Do you always get your way?"

A bleak look came over his face. "No. Not always," he said slowly. Crossing the room, he went to stand at the window. Minutes passed. Once, he turned back to her and started to say something, then stopped himself.

A nurse came in to check Jaclyn's pulse and to stick a

thermometer in her mouth. "I need your name for our records."

Jaclyn mumbled around the thermometer. The woman looked over at Shane, her eyebrows raised in question.

"Mrs. Gino Spinnelli," Shane said harshly. He started across the room toward the door.

"Mmno," Jaclyn mumbled, shaking her head. She removed the obstruction. "I said my name is Jaclyn Taylor."

Shane stopped, turned, and stared at her. Frowning, he walked toward her. "What—"

The doctor came in then, interrupting him, and he was asked to wait outside.

Jaclyn was sitting in a chair by the window when she heard the door open.

"Well?" Shane asked, coming over to pull a chair up beside her.

"The leg's fine, just as I told you. Shane, did—did he do something to my father's car, too?" she asked quietly.

Shane took her hand in his. "We don't know."

"It doesn't really matter, I don't suppose. I mean, it won't bring him back." She bit her lip to still its trembling.

"Jaclyn, I'm sorry, I really am. This must be a shock for you. Look, I don't want to leave you now. No, don't say you're fine, you're not. Listen, would it help if I tried to talk with the police and got the charges dropped if Gino left the country with—"

She stared at him, aghast. "Why would you do something like that?"

There was a knock at the door, then it was opened by the nurse. "Excuse me, Mr. Jaeger, but I'm supposed to tell you it's time."

"Time?" Shane said blankly.

"The race, remember?" Shaking her head disbelievingly, the woman closed the door.

"You go," Jaclyn told him. "I'm fine now. If you can just hand me my crutches, please?"

He stood, went for them, but stopped, his hands touching them absently, his back to her. "So this time I get a good-bye, then."

She lifted her shoulders in a helpless gesture. "I'm sorry I left like that. But I had to."

"Why?" He turned, the crutches forgotten, and she saw pain in his eyes. "I thought we had something." He walked over to the window and stared out unseeingly. "I hope you never go through this, Jaclyn. Never."

"What?" she asked, confused by his behavior.

He slammed his fist against the wall. "Loving—loving someone who doesn't return your love. I hope it never happens to you, although I don't think what Gino feels for you is love, or what you—" He stopped, unable to go on.

Jaclyn found herself getting to her feet, struggling across the space between them without her crutches. She touched his arm.

"Go away, Jaclyn. I hope—I hope he makes you happy." There was no bitterness in his voice now.

"He can't, Shane—"

"I know he can't!"

"Because I don't want him. I want *you*."

"Then why did you marry him?" He turned his head to look at her.

"What?"

He told her about seeing her and Gino at the church.

"So that *was* you. My mother got married that day. Not me."

"Then why did you leave Daytona?"

217

"I couldn't stay." Now it was she who had to turn away, unable to look at him as she talked. "I was afraid that you were just saying anything to keep me there. I was afraid that you didn't love me," she finished quickly, before she lost her nerve.

He pulled her to him, stood with her clasped so closely that she could feel his heart beating against her. "I fell in love with you from the start, almost from the moment I met you. I've never felt this way about a woman, do you know that?" He laughed, as if he couldn't believe it himself. "That's why I did anything I could do with the interview to keep you around for a while. I figured if I did, the attraction would wear off. You know what happened."

"Tell me. *Tell me.*"

"I had—I have to have you."

"You do, Shane. Oh, you do!" she cried, burying her face against his chest. "*Any* way. No promises. I don't care about anything else now. I just want to be with you, for however long."

"I love you," he said, his voice husky with emotion. "Let me show you how much." He lowered his mouth to hers with a muffled groan.

She wound her arms around his neck, ran her fingers through his dark hair as he pressed her so closely that she couldn't breathe and didn't care. When at last he released her lips she drew a long, shaky breath.

"What do you mean, no promises?" His warm breath fanned her cheek as his lips moved against the soft skin.

"I'll stay for as long as you want me, Shane."

"Forever?"

She unwound her arms and pulled back a little to stare up at him. "What?" she asked uncertainly.

"Did you really think I wouldn't make that promise?"

His eyes were warm with love, and desire, as he looked down at her. "I don't know whether to be honored or insulted. Marry me, Jaclyn. I love you, and I want your ring on my finger, joined by a piece of paper, bound so tightly to me that you won't ever think you can just run away and leave me, so that my life is no longer complete."

"Yes, Shane, yes!" She threw herself into his arms even closer, nearly unbalancing them both in her joy.

He pulled her down to sit on his lap, kissing her lips, her hair, the softness of her neck. His hands caressed her, bringing awake dormant memories of lovemaking on a stormy night, on a sun-filled morning. . . .

"Excuse me." It was the nurse again.

"No!" Shane growled.

Jaclyn sat up, blushing, and tried to bring some order to her appearance.

The nurse stared at the ceiling, trying hard to ignore Shane's continuing to kiss a protesting Jaclyn. "Uh, sir, there's an awful lot of people out here waiting for you."

"Shane! The race!" Jaclyn cried, struggling to get up.

He stopped her, his hands firm on her waist. "Jaclyn?"

"Yes, Shane," Jaclyn said simply. "Yes."

"Do you mean that? I'll understand if—"

"No." She cut off his words with a kiss. "You have to do this for yourself, and for me, too. If you don't get into that car today, if you never race, you'll always wonder if you could have, if your fear held you back. I have to conquer my fears, too. You go out there and win for both of us, do you hear me?"

"You win," he said, grinning. Then, growing serious, he touched her cheek with his hand. "You're first with me, *do you hear me? First,*" he repeated, and she knew he meant it. She'd never have to compete with the metal mistress for this man!

A short time later she sat in the section of the stands reserved for the drivers' families and guests and watched Shane pace beside his car, waiting for the race to begin. She knew he wasn't going to race against other men today. During their interview he'd told her how a true racer was in a contest with himself. She was testing herself today, too, seeing if she could let him do what he needed to do, to show him she truly loved him. And when the black car with a streak of silver down its length surged to the front of the pack and stayed there through the race, she didn't need a program to know it was Shane's car, didn't need to remember those were the colors of his uniform today. The driver of that car was bent on winning, wanted victory badly. His driving was sure, steady, just as were her nerves. Well, almost! she told herself when once or twice she found her heart in her throat when all the time she knew he was one of the best racers she'd ever watched. Her decision had been just as sure and right for both of them.

Mitch came to insist that Shane wanted Jaclyn with him in the winner's circle, and it was she who presented him with his trophy. Her reward for what she'd done, for her own private contest, came when he pulled her against him and kissed her so that the sounds of everything around them—the roar of the crowd's approval, the whirring of press cameras, the popping of champagne corks—faded into the distance. Something wet hit them. They drew apart and laughed when they found Mitch and the crew spraying the traditional winner's champagne over both of them. Their secret was out.

Back at the camper, when they'd finally managed to get

220

away from everyone, Shane drew Jaclyn into his arms again and kissed her hungrily. "Mmm, you taste of champagne." His voice was husky with desire. He pulled the collar of the damp shirt that clung revealingly to her body away from her neck, licking the drops of champagne from her skin. She shivered as his lips trailed lower, lower, as he peeled away her clothes, then his, pulling her down onto the bed.

There was a pounding on the camper door, and at first Jaclyn tried to make Shane aware of it. Then he was cutting off her words with his kisses, and she didn't care anymore that somebody wanted him, because she did—and he was hers, "exclusively" now—forever!

JAEGER CHEATS RIVAL, CLAIMS VICTORY IN RACE AND LOVE

—Jack Hathaway,
MOTOR SPORTS WRITER

NEW YORK—Actor-race driver Shane Jaeger is a lucky man.

But one of his victories won't be celebrated in victory lane, or win another Academy Award.

Jaeger announced his engagement to magazine journalist Jaclyn Taylor when he gave me an exclusive interview in the pit area after his startling win here at Bridghampton.

The normally press-shy Jaeger joked that he wasn't giving me an exclusive for the same purpose he had granted Ms. Taylor one recently.

"I fell in love with her at the twenty-four-hour Daytona race," he confessed, "and I tricked her into interviewing me so that I'd have the chance to ask her to marry me."

How does Ms. Taylor feel about his strategy to win her? I wanted to know.

"At least he can't say I led him a merry chase," the willowy blonde said with a smile. "He's promised, of course, that I'll get all his exclusive interviews from now on, and what journalist could resist that?"

What was it like interviewing the actor said to be more elusive than the legendary Garbo?

"Read about it in next month's issue of *Life-Styles*," Ms. Taylor said, displaying a little mystery of her own.

How did she feel about Jaeger's win in both a race and love in the same day?

It was a victory of sorts for her, too, she said, smiling at the actor, but she wouldn't elaborate.

They refused to answer questions about a dramatic pre-race incident in which international race driver Gino Spinnelli was arrested, saying that they had not yet given a statement to the police.

But I learned that Spinnelli will be charged with attempted murder for tampering with Jaeger's car before the race. Authorities are also investigating the cause of Jaeger's flaming crash at Daytona, in which he was injured. Spinnelli allegedly considered Jaeger to be a rival both in racing and for Ms. Taylor's affections, a police source close to the case said.

I asked Ms. Taylor how she felt about his racing.

"I won't ever try to stop him," she told me. "I've found that I don't have to compete with the metal mistress for this man."

Jaeger's pit crew interrupted us before I could ask what she meant, popping the traditional celebration champagne and dousing not just their driver [for the second time] but also his fiancée. A grinning Mitch Corbin, ex-stock car driver and friend and mentor of Jaeger's, had evidently tipped the crew off to the engagement.

I tried to get Ms. Taylor to explain her remark about a "metal mistress," but the two escaped well-wishers and press alike by retreating into Jaeger's camper.

As the parking lot emptied and my knocks on the camper door went unheeded, I remembered what Ms. Taylor had said about her lifelong rights to Shane Jaeger's exclusive interviews. I left the nearly empty racetrack.

It looks as though I'm no longer the only person in the press Shane Jaeger will allow to interview him. I guess I'll have to pick up a copy of that interview. . . .